Praise for Virginia Winters

The Facepainter Murders

"BOOK 2 IN A GREAT SERIES, from Virginia Winters, that will thrill mystery readers and genealogists alike. Masterful writing that puts all the clues before the reader, but hides them so the ending remains a surprise."

– Arline Chase, author of Ghost Dancer, Killraven, and the Spirit series, Spirit of Earth, Spirit of Fire, Spirit of Wind.

Murderous Roots

"FOUR STARS Recently widowed, Canadian doctor Anne McPhail takes leave to trace her genealogy. Ar- riving in a small Vermont town her ancestors once lived in, Anne discovers the body of the librarian she came to meet. Since the police suspect the dead woman may have been using her genealogy expertise to blackmail her clients, they ask Anne to help them reconstruct her research, uncovering several dangerous secrets before finally finding the murderer.

"An enjoyable read for genealogists as you experience Anne's elation when she finally finds the record she was searching for."

• Jane Nelson, Amazon Reviews

"FIVE STARS: Fun book, especially for a genealogist. There are many trails for the police to follow after a blackmailing librarian is murdered. The characters are interesting and the ones you think will wind up being suspects turn out to be just what they appear to be while others don't. I could not put it down."

• Mitzy Moo "Eclectic Reader" Amazon Reviews

"FOUR STARS: A clever murder mystery with a window into Canadiana, a small town librarian feels compelled to investigate what appears to be a simple murder.... but clearly isn't. Our unlikely heroine finds her self in the midst of intrigue, danger, and of course some romance. Written with just the right amount of attention to detail and interspersed with wit and humor, this book should be entertaining for both mystery lovers and genealogy enthusiasts alike."

• J. Summers (Florida), Amazon Reviews

"FOUR STARS: Whoever said the life of a small-town librarian must be dull? As cadavers pile up, large sums of money change hands, deliberate "accidents" are narrowly averted and romances begin to blossom, the local police are still no wiser. It's time for an amateur genealogist to step in and help solve the mystery."

• Nancy Pratt (France), Amazon Reviews

THE FACEPAINTER MURDERS

VIRGINIA WINTERS

From the River Publishing

THE FACEPAINTER MURDERS
DANGEROUS JOURNEYS SERIES, VOL. 2
by Virginia Winters

From The River Publishing

Cover Design by Karen Phillips © 2017

❀ Created with Vellum

For my family

Preface

In the early years of the 21st century, genealogical information on the internet exploded with data available from multiple resources. Readers familiar with genealogy will note that most of those resources are not referenced in this book, which was written before they became available.

Acknowledgments

Thanks to my friend, Barbara McFadzen, for the many Friday nights she has spent listening to me while I read the latest story or chapter to her.

Thanks are due to the Lindsay Public Library, reference division for its invaluable help.

Finally, thanks to editor Shelley Rodgerson Chase for all the extra hours she spent on the first edition of The Facepainter Murders.

Chapter One

Maggie danced around the body that lay face down in the muddy water remaining in the ditch after the afternoon rain. Anne grabbed the dog's collar and dragged her away from her find. She smelled it all the way from the house, she thought. That's why she was so frantic to get out here.

She squatted by the head. A precise hole, visible in the tangled mass of blood and hair, marked an entry point above the right ear. No point in touching him, she thought. No point but someone would ask if she made sure he was dead. Her fingers felt through the water for his carotid pulse. Nothing. Nothing except that smell. Fighting the waves of nausea that threatened to overwhelm her, she wiped her fingers on the grassy bank and stood up.

"That's enough."

She hauled Maggie through the gate onto the path. The protesting dog tugged the length of the garden and up to the kitchen door.

Catherine swung around from the stove when the screen door slammed behind Anne.

"There's a body in the ditch."

Anne collapsed into a kitchen chair, out of breath from her tug-of-war with the dog.

"Who?"

"I don't know. How could I? I just got here; remember? Eighteen months since I was here last, and in all that time, did I find a body at home? No. Cross the border and here's another one, waiting for me in your back garden."

The ghost of a smile at the lame joke crossed Catherine's pale face.

"I'll call 911. No ambulance?"

"Yes, he's gone. As are all his clothes. Whoever left him there took all his clothes away."

"Naked?"

"Absolutely. I should go back. You're supposed to stay with a body."

Anne slumped against a pillar, watching the orange and black of an Oriole as it darted at the feeder. The garden was a mass of scarlet and ochre with brilliant strokes of indigo from the butterfly bushes. Far better, she thought, to stay here. The dog whined from the other side of the screen door. Behind her, Catherine spoke quickly to the 911 operator.

"No, Maggie," she said as she hung up the phone.

Anne forced herself off the porch and through the garden as far as the gate. She didn't go through but stood to look at the fields while she waited for the patrol car and the questions. There would be many questions, that, she knew. When she had found the murdered librarian on her last visit here, they'd been endless. She became involved with the investigation, and then she had almost died. Almost been killed. It had taken many months for the night-mares to stop.

She waited by the body. The wind had picked up, rippling the water and giving an illusion of movement as it disturbed a few strands of the dark hair. She shivered in the sudden chill as the sun fell below the trees. The wail of a siren, rising and falling in the distance, came closer and stopped when the patrol car turned into the lane. The murky water, reddened by the flashing lights, lapped the body as though it steeped in its blood. She shivered again as she turned to the voices of the policemen who walked towards her.

"Hi, Dr. McPhail," said the taller of the two men, Dave Graham.

Anne met Dave and his older brother, Pete on her previous visit.

"Damn shame you have to find a body every time you come down to Vermont," said Pete, more lighthearted than his serious younger brother.

"Was he dead when you got here?" asked Dave.

"Yes. I smelled him, and so did the dog. That's why I came back here. The dog. She wanted to see what it was."

"Do you recognize him?"

"No."

"How long have you been in the country, Doctor?"

"I arrived yesterday."

Pete stood back as Dave asked the questions. Maybe he thought he knew her too well. Everyone's a suspect until they're not, she remembered Adam saying to her.

"Okay, you go back to the house now. Adam will be along to speak to you," Dave said to her as Pete muttered into his shoulder radio.

"All right."

Anne walked back through the garden, not noticing the few flowers picked out by the last rays of the sun.

Catherine was pouring tea into gaily-painted ceramic mugs when Anne opened the screen door.

"Do you want something to eat while we wait for Adam?"

"I don't think I can. How do you know I'm waiting for Adam?"

Catherine laughed.

"Culver's is a small town, with one detective who investigates homicides. Besides, when the patrolman reported who found the body, Adam would come anyway. After all the help you were to him the last time you were here, I'm sure he wants to see you again."

"Dave Graham didn't seem as friendly as last time. He seemed quite suspicious."

"Don't worry. Adam knows you."

"Yes, but two bodies in as many years?"

Catherine didn't answer but turned to fill her teapot.

"What is it?" Anne asked as she watched Catherine's fingers turn white where they encircled her cup.

"Not the best advertisement for a bed and breakfast," she said, her eyes filling with sudden tears. "It's all I have, and the twins are going away to school next year."

Catherine's husband died in the second year of their marriage, leaving her with the twins, the big old house and enough insurance money to bury him and start her business.

"Should I go look at him? What if he's someone I know? What if he's been a guest here?"

Now the cup shook. Anne reached over and held Catherine's hands. Cold, she thought. She needs her hot drink.

"Wait until they come for us. Please drink your tea. You're very cold."

An hour later, Anne waited for Adam in Catherine's little library. She left her little grey brick house in Bridgenorth, a small town in Ontario, the day before, leaving behind her Siamese cat, Albert. She considered bringing him this year but wasn't sure how Maggie would feel about a cat invading her domain. Maggie sat on her footstool, as usual, surveying her from behind grey bushy eyebrows. Half sheepdog, she needed to keep all her humans in sight. When Adam came in, she welcomed him with a few thumps of her slightly too short tail.

"Hey, Maggie," he said, rubbing her ears. "Hello, Anne."

His dark eyes and thin face looked more relaxed than last year, she thought, not as edgy. Catherine said that he was still seeing

Erin, a local antique dealer.

"Adam, I didn't hear the doorbell."

"I came through the kitchen. How are you?"

"Not too bad, considering."

"Tell me about it."

Anne told him about finding the body. "...and Maggie pushed ahead of me, so there will be dog prints. I hauled her out of there as soon as I was sure the man was dead."

"Did you see or hear anything else?"

"No. We heard a car in the lane before Maggie started barking, but no one was around when I went out."

Adam settled back in his chair and looked at her: small, early forties, fair hair, green eyes set in a round face which bore an unexpected tan. She was a little thinner than last year, more grey in the fair hair, and a little tired-looking. Finding bodies could do that to you. He hoped neither she nor Catherine had any connection to the dead man. Anne was talking.

"I've been so looking forward to this trip. I hope you'll have dinner with me."

"I hope so too."

He held out a small plastic bag with a torn scrap of paper in it.

"Do you recognize this?"

"Is it part of a ticket? I've not seen one like that, but I only got here yesterday."

"We found it in the guy's hand."

"What a strange thing to hold on to."

Adam stood up.

"Yes, it was. Catherine had to view the body. I hear them in the kitchen. Maybe she needs you."

Catherine did indeed need her. Her thin body trembled and her dark eyes held a film of tears. Anne sat with her arm around Catherine until she stopped shaking.

"Catherine, did you know him?" Adam asked.

"No, I've never seen him before. Inhuman, somehow, to abandon him in a ditch."

She looked across the table at Adam. "I don't think he's local."

"Neither do I. Thanks, ladies and thank you, Maggie."

He rubbed the ears of the worried-looking dog, sitting with her head on Catherine's knee, walked out into the night, and across the garden to where the crew worked.

The forensics crew searched the lane and the roadside, moving like shadows in and out of the lights set up around the scene. The body was dumped, Adam thought. Why would he have a ticket in his hand if he saw the attack coming? What was the ticket for? After a few words with Pete, he drove back through town to the police station.

The station was part of the courthouse complex on one side of the town square. Culver's Mills, population seventeen thousand, was a post-card-typical Vermont small town. The courthouse, clock tower and police station formed one side of the square. Opposite stood the white clapboard Methodist church. A short row of shops, including an antique store owned by Erin Maxwell—his special lady —and professional offices filled in one side; a restaurant, homes and the bank, the other. Brick pathways crisscrossed a small green space, centered on a heroic statue of the town's founder. Quelling the impulse to stop and see Erin, he parked in front of the court-house and took the ten steps to the door two at a time.

The police station occupied one wing of the courthouse build-ing. The court's side was all polished marble floors and dark oak paneling, but once through the station doors, only the bright screensavers on the desk computers enlivened the institutional-green walls, grey vinyl floors and steel filing cabinets. Four desks were jammed in the middle of the room. Cables, secured to the floor with duct tape, snaked around and between them.

"Brad," Adam said to his youngest officer, a computer expert.

"Yeah, boss."

Brad was tall and loosely put together, his friendly nature showing all over his face.

"We have a problem. Our stiff out there has no clothes, no id. We'll need the fingerprints, dental impressions, maybe an artist. I don't think he'll photograph too well."

"I'll borrow from Burlington if we need one. Was there anything else at the scene?"

"This."

Adam showed him the torn ticket. He noticed now that the two letters remaining were Cu suggesting it was for something in town.

"Not like any ticket I've seen lately. I'll get a list of recent events from the paper and the rec center. Bars too. Sometimes they use tickets for bands."

Brad picked up his phone to start his round of calls.

"Circulate the motels and B and B's for missing guests and get the boys to check any abandoned vehicles. I'm going over to talk to Peg."

"Will do," Brad said.

Peg was the owner of the local diner, Lil's, and it was dinner time.

The diner sat diagonally across the square from the courthouse in an old stone building that had previous lives as a lumberman's office and a grocery store but was Lil's for the last fifty years.

Adam walked past the statue in the middle of the park, automatically touching the toe for luck as he passed, and up the stairs to the door. Lil herself was long gone, but the décor remained the same. Red vinyl seats in comfortable booths filled the space in front of the windows on three sides. A white enamel counter, worn through to black in a few places, ran the length of the room. An old-fashioned, polished chrome milkshake maker stood at one end of the counter. Adam took one of the red and chrome stools and said hello to Peg.

"Hi, Adam—usual?"

Peg herself was thoroughly modern: close-cropped sandy hair, a pair of rimless glasses and a white shirt tied short over faded jeans.

"Sure."

Peg made the best chicken salad sandwiches, from her home-reared and home-cooked chickens he'd had anywhere, and he tried them everywhere. He looked around the room, recognizing everyone except a family with two kids who were enjoying themselves, spinning around on the stools. No singles.

"Do you know who he is yet?" asked Peg when she brought him the food.

"Don't tell me the news is around already."

"I'm afraid so."

"No identification yet. Have there been many strangers through this week?"

"A few. Most people were families or couples. Early in the week, a guy asked about art galleries and antique stores. I sent him across to Erin."

"What did he look like?"

Adam reached for the catsup for his fries.

"About six feet, brown hair and eyes, small tight ears, straight nose, good teeth. Spoke well but he was pushy."

"Could be our guy. You don't remember a name or a vehicle?"

"Didn't hear a name and I didn't see him get in a car. He walked over to Erin's after his lunch."

"Thanks. How's your sister?"

Adam knew that Peg's sister May suffered from severe rheumatoid arthritis.

"Much better. Since we got the money from the trust, you know, we moved to the farm, all one floor and we got her some first-class care."

Last year, as fallout from a murder case, Adam identified May and Peg as beneficiaries of a local family trust.

"Has the family been decent?"

"Couldn't have been nicer or more welcoming. We keep a distance, but they've been good to us."

"Why are you still here?" Adam asked, suspecting the answer he got.

"I enjoy it, especially the gossip."

Adam laughed, paid, and left to visit Erin.

The lights were on upstairs in Erin's building though the shop was dark. Adam went around the side and rang the bell. The intercom that he insisted she install crackled a moment before he heard her voice asking who was there.

"It's me," he said with the softness that crept into his voice when he spoke to her. The lock snapped open as she told him to come up. He took the stairs two at a time to reach where she stood, silhouetted against the light from her apartment.

Erin was tall enough that her dark hair brushed his chin. Dark brown eyes accentuated the pale complexion of her oval face. Adam kissed her softly, and they walked together into her apartment. Erin called it her loft although her bed stood in a screened alcove and not visible from the living area. The large room took up most of the second floor of the house. One wall held a brick and tile fireplace surrounded by old pine bookshelves. Erin changed the furniture often, swapping pieces with her shop. Today she had a green corduroy overstuffed sofa and chair—his favorites.

"What's the matter?"

"You know Anne's here to visit? She's found another body."

"Oh, no. Who is it?"

"We don't know. He was naked, and nothing was around him to identify him except this."

He showed her the ticket fragment, but she shook her head slowly no.

"Peg said she sent a stranger who was interested in art galleries and antiques over to see you. Tall, she said, brown hair and eyes, pushy?"

"Oh, yes. Tuesday. I remember him because he demanded to see any paintings I had stored away. I told him what I had was in the shop and he was welcome to browse. What I wanted to do was throw him out."

Adam grinned at the thought of fierce little Erin throwing the guy out. Aloud he said, "Did you get a name?"

"John."

"Just John?"

"Just John. He didn't buy anything, so I don't have a check or a credit slip or anything."

"Will you look at a picture when I get one? It won't be too nice."

"Sure."

Erin's face had grown paler. Adam put his arm around her and started talking about their upcoming vacation. In a few months, he and Erin planned a trip to Bermuda—sun and relaxation and each other.

Their conversation was interrupted by a call telling Adam that the body was being moved from the crime scene to the morgue.

"Back to work."

He got up from the sofa and stretched. A quick kiss and he was gone.

Chapter Two

The smell of freshly-baked bread nudged Anne awake from a sleep troubled by nightmares of bodies and bloodstained water. After she showered, she put on a pair of jeans and a heavy Arran cable knit sweater in her favorite soft violet color. It would be a cold walk to the library.

She opened the door at the bottom of the back stairs to the kitchen. Catherine stood at the old range, frying bacon and quietly crying. She wiped her face with the corner of her apron as Anne came in.

"Has something else happened?" Anne asked.

"Adam questioned the boys, and Mrs. Adams checked out, and it will be all over town, and people will talk. They'll say he was my lover and he was killed in my house. What am I going to do?"

Anne put her arms around the shaking shoulders, and made soothing sounds and patted Catherine's back.

"Adam will find the killer, and then it will be clear the crime had nothing to do with you. He had to question the twins, but they played basketball in Brownsville all weekend, didn't they?"

"Yes."

"I'm sure the time of death will clear them of all suspicion. Mrs.

Adams was an old fusspot and more trouble than she was worth. We'll get Peg at the diner to spread the word the body was dumped in the lane, not on your property. She can talk if she wants to."

"How do you know the body was dumped?"

"Not much blood and there were tracks in the lane."

They stood at the window and looked out over the garden. Frost had touched the flowers that glistened in the early morning sun. Birds flitted to and from the feeder. Catherine's shoulders relaxed, and Anne took her arm away.

"Do you think I could have some of that lovely bacon?"

"Oh, of course."

Catherine returned to the familiar routine of feeding a guest, and Anne to eating the substantial breakfast Catherine offered to help her guests get through their day.

The art gallery housed a travelling exhibit of colonial paintings in the library Anne wanted to view. After breakfast, and satisfied Catherine was calmer, she walked the few blocks towards the town square.

The octagonal, red-brick library and its glass and stone addition sat back from the street in a small park outlined by a black wrought-iron fence. A new herringbone-patterned brick walk led to the front door, but the plaque on the wall, dating it to 1912 and identifying Andrew Carnegie as the benefactor, remained.

Anne walked up the three cut-stone steps and pushed on the oak door's brass plate, worn from a century of hands, and went upstairs to the gallery in the addition.

The door stood open, although the sign said the show was over. A few paintings still hung on the pale yellow walls of the long gallery, illuminated by a single large window behind the volunteers' table, and a complicated series of pot-lights and track-lighting on the ceiling. Old-fashioned faces stared back at her as she looked around the room. Blank spaces marked the missing paintings that a young girl, working near the back exit, wrapped and inserted into crates.

"Hello, Anne. Welcome back to Culver's Mills," said the grey-haired volunteer smiling up at her from her table.

Anne recognized Ada Warren, a retired teacher and local history authority.

"Thank you, Ada. I hope I'm in time to see some of the paintings?"

"Oh, yes. I'll ask Chrissy to stop wrapping."

Ada was using a cane this year, a change for an active woman who had been an avid bowler and gardener.

"No fee?" said Anne, glancing at a roll of tickets on the desk.

"Not today."

Ada walked down the room and spoke to the young girl who bounced up and out.

"I hope the cane isn't permanent?" Anne asked when she returned.

"Oh no, I twisted my ankle trying roller-blading."

She strolled with Anne down the gallery, pausing to look at each picture that remained on view. The details of the painting—the background, the clothing, the furniture and other smaller details helped place a portrait in time. Some were memorial with different figures in the landscape representing aspects of the subject's life. They stopped in front of the portrait of a young woman standing with one hand resting on the back of an ornately carved chair.

"My great-great-grandmother," Ada said.

"You look like her."

Anne noted the long, oval face and the upward slant to the smoky blue eyes. The artist captured the playful nature of the subject despite the serious pose.

"She was one of the early teachers in the school here, and married the first mayor of Culver's Mills."

"And you carry on the family tradition?"

Ada had taught history at the local high school for thirty years.

"Yes, except for the marrying the mayor portion."

Ada was the widow of a long-serving judge. Of the paintings that were missing, two, in particular, would have been of interest to Anne, she said.

"Except for the one of Ada Deacon, my ancestor, the other local painting was that of a man whose family has long since died out. We have a sampler worked as a family register by a later family member."

"Where are the paintings going?"

"To Brownsville, a town about a hundred miles south of here. We're shipping them this evening, but those two have local owners so perhaps another time."

"Whose are they?"

"They belong to Evan's. You know—the restaurant?"

"Oh, yes."

"The subject of the painting, Samuel Hall, a goldsmith, quite a well-known one, who lived in Boston was born in the house, and when he died, some of his belongings were sent back here to his sister. Zedekiah Belknap painted his portrait."

Anne laughed.

"What a delightfully eccentric name. Who was he?"

"Quite a well-known face-painter or limner. He worked in New England all of his life and lived here in Vermont for much of it," Ada said. "You're familiar with limners?"

"Weren't they itinerant artists who travelled from village to village, painting the members of families, in the days before photography."

"Yes, that's right. A museum in New Hampshire sent us the sampler. It was worked by a later descendant of the Halls. It's framed in intricately carved mahogany and stitched in silk on linen, with a border of exquisite flowers. It had been locked away for many years, and the colors are very fresh."

"Sounds beautiful and valuable, too."

"Oh, I think so. We had to pay a lot to insure this show, especially with the Belknap and the museum piece in it."

After some further discussion of the economics of running

small-town art galleries and fund-raising, Anne left to walk back to Catherine's. She stood for a moment on the steps of the library, with the nagging feeling that she had ignored something important. Knowing that it would eventually come to her, she shook her head and strolled on.

Chapter Three

"Any word back on the prints?" Adam asked Pete when he walked into the squad room that afternoon.

"Not yet, but we're still waiting for Interpol."

Pete was roaming the squad room from computer to fax and back.

"Why can't these guys get back to us sooner."

"Don't forget the RCMP and the Sûreté."

Close as they were to the Canadian border, Pete never remembered the police services north of the line.

"No record of him in the motels?"

"We're still checking."

Pete sat down at his desk to write another fax.

"Something else, boss?"

"No. I was thinking how much easier it would all be if the hotels had to report on their guests every night, the way the French had it in the past."

"Like people here would put up with that."

"Yeah."

"The sheriff over in Brownsville called. You know that art show that was at the library?" Brad said.

"No."

"The paintings left last night by courier to Brownsville and arrived today. They're reporting that two of the paintings are missing. Someone wrapped up blank canvases and frames and substituted them for the originals."

"They think it happened here?"

"Or between here and there. Thing is the company that moved them specializes in this, and they insist that they delivered what they picked up. Each piece had a seal."

"Someone stole them from the library here. The library again."

Erin had directed the dead man to the library. Perhaps a connection, he thought.

"Okay, let's get over there."

Brad stayed with the vehicle while Adam took the stairs to the gallery. The notice on the door said it was closed until the next week. On his way out, he stopped at the chief librarian's office door and knocked.

"Morning, Nancy."

He had gone to school with Nancy Webb, a tall blustery woman with an aggressive tone of voice. They didn't get along then and didn't now, especially since her assistant had turned up dead in the middle of the library floor last year. Adam took Nancy's computers into evidence, and she resented it.

"Hello, Adam. What is it this morning?"

Nancy walked out from behind her desk to meet him at her door.

"Theft. Two of the paintings from upstairs were stolen. They never arrived in Brownsville."

"Well. The library is not my responsibility. It does have separate management and director."

"The security isn't. Have you had any problems?"

"One of those silly teenage volunteers forgot to set it last night." Nancy turned back to her desk and sat.

"Which one?"

"Chrissy."

"Did you notify us?"

"Of course not. Nothing was missing."

"There's something missing now, and you're supposed to call us."

"I can't call you every time one of those foolish teenagers forgets to do what's she's told."

"Yeah, you can. Where can I find this Chrissy?"

"I have no idea. Ask Ada. Those girls are her pets."

"Is she here?"

"I have no idea."

The woman at the desk did and told Adam that Ada had gone home.

Adam walked down the few steps to the front door and out to his car. Nancy stared after him, running both hands through her mousy-brown hair, her long face impassive.

Ada's red-brick home stood back from the street, its front garden surrounded by a picketed wrought-iron fence. Adam parked on the street and walked up the flagstone walk to the front door. When there was no answer to his rings, he followed the path, under a rose arbor and through an arched white gate to the back garden.

Ada, her tall, elegant figure dressed in jeans and work boots, was dumping bags of leaves onto her flower beds, helped by a pony-tailed, teenage girl. Ada's cane was hooked over the branch of a near-bye tree.

"Morning, Ada."

She was one of Adam's favorites, his high school history teacher and mentor.

"Good morning, Adam. Do you know Chrissy Chambers?"

Perky described Chrissy, he thought, as she said, "Lieutenant Davidson, I presume." Or maybe cheeky. Cheerful.

"Hi, Chrissy. I'm glad you're here. I'd like to talk to both of you."

"Come in the kitchen. What's the matter?" Ada said as she led the way, stopping to remove her dirt-laden boots.

While they sat at the well-scrubbed pine kitchen table, Adam asked about the paintings.

"Chrissy, did you wrap all the paintings for travel?"

"No."

"No?" said Ada.

"No, I didn't. I thought that you started before I came. Two of them were already wrapped. The ones at the end."

Both looked at Adam, more perplexed than worried.

"Did you set the alarm?" Adam said

"Yes, I did. No matter what that old witch Nancy Webb says. I set it like Mrs. Warren showed me. She trusts me. That's why she lets me close. Isn't it, Mrs. Warren?"

She turned a face threatening to cry, to her teacher.

"Nancy got you in trouble, did she?"

"Yes, but I didn't do anything wrong."

"Chrissy's a reliable girl," Ada said.

"Can either of you remember anyone coming more than once or behaving in a way that drew you attention?"

Ada sat back in her chair, shaking her head.

"I didn't spend time looking at the visitors during the week."

"I did," said Chrissy. "Some were strange, like that guy who wanted to copy the picture. He wanted to set up his easel and paint right in the middle of all the other visitors. Do you remember?" she said, turning to Mrs. Warren. "He was angry when Mrs. Fox said he couldn't."

"Mrs. Fox?"

"Our director. I can give you her number."

"He came back two more times. Once to take pictures, and Mrs. Fox said no again, and then on the day before and on the last day, too," Chrissy said.

"What did he look like?"

"Oh, I don't know. He was an older guy, tall, sort of plain."

"Did you see anyone else come more that once?"

"Oh, sure," said Chrissy, as she shifted her chair closer to Adam. "Erin Maxwell from the antique store, she came three times, and the librarian, she came every day and that old guy who lives out in the Scott house. He was really creepy."

Chrissy paused to take a breath.

"Stop, Chrissy. Who is this old guy? Ada?" he asked.

"James Trevelyan. He claims to be descended from the people who owned the house Evan's is in. The family was called Hall. Incidentally, Hall was the subject of the missing portrait. Nancy came by daily on her way to the reference section as part of her rounds. She always does it."

"Okay. You say the portrait was of this Hall?"

"Yes. The sampler was an early record of the family. The family has died out, so I'm not sure Trevelyan is a descendant.

"What did he do, Chrissy? Why was he so weird?"

Chrissy tossed her hair and rolled her eyes.

"He came and sat in front of that painting all morning and didn't move. Three mornings. I think he made everyone nervous. All the other people would sneak past him, and he would make a rude noise, sort of a growl, if someone stood in front of him too long."

"Anyone else?"

"No."

"Thank you, ladies."

∾

Two unusual crimes in one week, Adam thought, as he drove towards the station. There wasn't any evidence that they were connected except the possibility that Chrissy's old plain guy was their corpse. Why such interest in those paintings? Why was Erin in so often? Might as well ask her, he said to himself as he drove into the parking space in front of the shop. Erin waved to him as he came in. She was ringing up a sale.

"Hi," she said as she showed her customers out. "Strange time of day for you. Come in and have some tea."

"Thanks." Adam twisted his hat in his hands. "Erin, I want to ask you a question."

"What are you embarrassed about?"

Erin smiled up at him.

"Ask."

"Okay. Why did you go back to the art show in the library three times?"

"Why? Who told you I did and why do you care?"

Her voice rose.

A volunteer called Chrissy. I have to check everyone who did anything unusual. Two of them were stolen."

"And so you come here to ask me like I might be a thief."

Erin's voice choked with anger.

"No, I came to ask so no gossip could say I ignored it. Try to understand."

Adam put his arm around her, but she shrugged him away. He stood in silence, watching her rigid back. Color rose on her neck, and when she turned back to answer him, bright blotches covered her cheeks and forehead.

"I guess you had to. I went once to take art gallery members around on opening day, once to a lunch for the volunteers and once for myself. Is that explanation enough?"

"Of course it is. Please, Erin."

"Go, go. Talk to me later."

Goddamit, he thought. Who cares what people thought? Why did he ask her? He would mend fences later. They fought so little that he didn't have much experience with her anger. The crackle of the radio interrupted his thoughts.

"Adam, Pete. We got something from the police in Montreal. Are you coming in?"

"I'll be right there."

Pete was sitting at his desk, staring at a fax.

"Hey, boss. Here's our man. He's an art thief."

"The theft over at the library may be connected. Did you say this info came from the Mounties?"

"No, Montreal. He's been operating there, but they haven't been able to arrest him. He runs a gallery that acts legit, but they suspect he fences and does some jobs, including international ones, himself."

Adam looked at the picture. The dark hair and tight little ears were those of the dead man.

"What's his name?"

"John Andrews."

"Not French?"

"No."

"Make some copies and try to trace him. You and Brad and Dave. I have to talk to the Captain. Give me a picture of the guy before you go."

Jim Naismith had been Chief of Police here for twenty years. Lately, he had been spending much of his time on a plan for more efficient integration of town and county forces, leaving the day-to-day to Adam. Silver-haired, blue eyes looking over half-glasses and a powerful physique running a bit to fat: Jim was still an imposing figure.

"Adam, what can I do for you?"

"Do you have time to talk over this homicide?"

"Sure. What do you have so far?"

Adam reported the murder, the identification of the victim and possible tie-in with the thefts from the gallery.

"What are the boys doing?"

"Trying to trace his movements."

"And you?"

"I think I'll go interview Jim Trevelyan."

"Okay, report when you can."

That's what Adam liked about Naismith—he gave him a free hand. Failure was all his too.

A man, leaning against the low wall that surrounded the parking lot, smoking at the courthouse doors, butted out and strode over to catch Adam as he reached his car. Ted Atkins worked for the local newspaper and covered court and police news.

"Hey, Lieutenant."

"Yeah? What do you want, Ted? I'm in a hurry," Adam said to the reporter as he opened the car door.

"What's going on at Catherine's. I heard you picked up a body."

"Where were you? I usually find you right behind the medical examiner."

"Out of town. Who was the dead guy? How did he die? Any suspects?"

"Not identified. Nothing further on it today. Gotta go."

Adam climbed into his car, leaving a chagrined Ted staring after him.

The road out to the farm called the old Scott place wound through wooded hills south from Culver's Mills. A sugarbush ran for miles on both sides of the road, interrupted by an occasional split-rail fence. In the spring, flexible yellow pipeline snaked from tree to tree, gathering the sap for the maple syrup producers. The crowns of the maple trees blazed scarlet and orange, with an occasional highlight of yellow. The ten-minute drive brought him to Trevelyan's fenced acreage.

A new electric gate, outfitted with an intercom, blocked the road into the property. Odd, Adam thought, not much of this kind of security around here. Wonder what he had to protect or hide? Adam pushed the big green button and waited. Nothing. He pushed again.

An angry, elderly voice came from the speaker.

"Who is it?"

"Police for James Trevelyan."

"How do I know you're police?"

"I'm Lieutenant Adam Davidson of Culver's Mills Police. You could let me in and look at my identification or call the station."

"I'll call the station."

A long five minutes later and the intercom spoke again. "They say you should be here, so come up, but I've got a shotgun."

"Are you threatening me, Mr. Trevelyan?"

"No, but if you aren't who you say you are, I'm warning you."

Adam put the red police light on top of his car and went through the gate, letting the siren announce his arrival. A long lane through the trees led to a two-story white house. Boards covered all but two windows on the ground floor. Trevelyan stood on the porch, at the top of the few stairs, the shotgun cradled in his arms.

"Mr. Trevelyan, I'm not walking up there with you pointing a shotgun at me. Now there's been a theft and a murder, and I need to talk to you. Put the gun down."

Indecision played over the old man's face until he propped the gun against a pillar and sat down on one of a pair of ladder-back chairs pushed against the house wall.

Adam walked up to him, his hands away from his body, one

holding his identification. The old man peered at it, took his glasses off, wiped his eyes with a voluminous red handkerchief that he took from the pocket of his baggy pants, and told Adam to sit down.

"Why all the security, Mr. Trevelyan?"

"Well, son, I've had a lot of trouble in my life, and now that I have a little property and expecting some more, I don't want anyone to take it from me. You said something about a theft and a murder. What's missing and who's dead and why are you asking me?"

"A man called John Andrews is dead. The two pictures you were most interested in at the library gallery have been stolen."

"What." The old man's face turned an alarming purple, and his neck swelled. "Those are my pictures. Who took them?"

"I don't know. Why do you claim them? I thought they belonged to the owners of Evan's."

"Ha. They found them in the house they bought. The house, the contents, the pictures are all mine. I have the will, and I inherit everything."

Now he was pacing up and down the porch, thumping his cane with each angry step.

"Could you tell me all about this?" Adam suggested quietly, hoping to calm the agitated old man.

"I'll show you. Come in. Come in."

He stomped into the house, forgetting the shotgun. Adam carried it inside. Hooks over the stone fireplace suggested where it ought to go. After shaking out the shells, he hung it up.

Trevelyan had disappeared. An old pine table gleamed in the afternoon sunshine, and an assortment of maple and pine chairs cramped the room. Adam flicked a wall switch. No electricity, so the oil-lamp on the table wasn't part of the décor. Odd, electricity to the gate but none in here, he thought. He sat at the table and waited.

The florid-faced old man wheezed as he sat down beside Adam, clutching a folder of papers.

"Here they are."

"Mr. Trevelyan, are you all right? Do you have some medicine you should be taking?"

"No medicine. I'll be all right. Read, man, read."

He thumped the documents with one gnarled fist.

The folder held a photocopy of an old will and a chart that Adam recognized as a family tree, as well as birth certificates, marriage certificates and what seemed to be several death records.

"I take it you claim to be descended from Samuel Hall."

"I don't claim it, I am. Can't you read? Look at the will."

Trevelyan's hands shook as he shuffled through the papers, putting first one and then another in front of Adam and as quickly snatching it away.

"Here it is. See. The will makes it clear."

Ornate lettering on a fragile, yellowed parchment proclaimed it to be the last will and testament of Samuel Hall, 1825. The paragraphs that followed, in antique prose and faded copperplate script, held that all the possessions of Samuel Hall, goldsmith, including a house, contents, portrait, and silver objects, were bequeathed to his sister, Charity, wife of Alexandre Leclerc, of Culver's Mills. In it, Adam read, he also wished her a long and happy life and forgave her for her conversion to Roman Catholicism.

"Do you have documents that go back from you to Hall or his sister?"

"Neither. I haven't traced it all the way with documents. My grandmother told me the story from her grandmother. I will prove it."

Agitated, he was pacing now, his limp more troublesome, and his wheezing louder.

"Perhaps I could take your file with me to show to a genealogy expert who is visiting Culver's Mills?"

"No."

He clutched the folder and glared at Adam.

"No one can have them."

"She wouldn't keep them. She would help you."

"No. Maybe I could bring them to her tomorrow so she could review them."

"Okay, come to the courthouse at ten. I'll ask Dr. McPhail to be there."

"Doctor. I don't need a doctor," he said.

"She knows about this genealogy stuff. Anyway, she's a children's doctor," Adam said.

"All right. I'll come tomorrow but now get the hell out of here."

The old man sat down at his table, sorting and caressing his documents. He didn't look up when Adam closed the door. Adam considered Trevelyan's potential as a killer. He was certainly capable of anger, but if the shotgun was his only weapon, he didn't kill Andrews. Ballistics had reported that he had been shot with a small caliber pistol, likely a Derringer DS22, not a common weapon in Culver's Mills. Trevelyan had seemed surprised and outraged at the missing art works. Placing Andrews at the gallery and Erin's was next. Possibly Chrissy could identify the picture if she had noticed the "plain guy's" face. Erin would. She had a good memory for faces.

Erin. He had better stop to talk to her. He took one of the two parking spaces behind the shop and walked around to the front. He held the door for a customer who was leaving with a small tapestry-covered footstool in hand. Inside the door, he paused to let his eyes adjust to the lower light level and looked around for Erin.

She sat, surrounded by invoices and statements, in an over-stuffed chair that had square arms and back. Fuzzy wine-coloured material upholstered the piece. A free-standing ashtray, all gleaming chrome with a horse mounted on the handle, blond coffee-table and end-table completed today's ensemble. Erin's head jerked when he spoke.

"Adam, I didn't hear you come in. Sit down."

Adam stayed standing where he was, turning his Stetson-style hat over and over.

"First, I'm sorry, Erin. I shouldn't have questioned you."

"Yes, you should have. I'm sorry I was so foolish. Sit down."

She held out her hands to him and pulled him down into a long embrace.

At length, they began to talk again.

"What is this stu—furniture, Erin?"

"1950's. I think it's the next thing. Do you like it?"

"It's comfortable and big, so yes I do. But 1950's isn't antique, is it?"

"There's a market for well-made furniture from any time. Some people are talking about anything over fifty years being antique, but I won't sell it that way, just as collectable."

"Will you look at a picture for me?" he said as he took it from an envelope.

"How gruesome is it?"

"Not. It's a picture from Motor Vehicles."

"That will be gruesome," she said. "Sure."

She examined the face in the picture.

"That's John," she said, "The fellow who was interested in my paintings. Is he the one?"

"Yes. Do you know where he went from here?"

"I told him about the show at the library and a few paintings in the capital building in Montpelier. I imagine that he went to the library the next day because it was too late when he left here."

"Did he say where he was staying?"

"No."

"What do you think the values of the painting and the sampler are?"

"The sampler is easy. About eight thousand dollars at auction. The painting is more difficult. It's a very good Belknap, but it doesn't have children in it, and the ones that do are the most popular. On the other hand, the colors are well preserved, and it's decorative. In 1995 a Belknap sold for one hundred and eighty-six thousand dollars. I would think maybe seventy-five thousand for this one as it is the most elaborate Belknap I have ever seen, but it depends. It could go for six thousand."

"Seventy-five thousand dollars. I didn't know anything as valuable as that was there. We're supposed to be informed. Were the rest as valuable?"

"No. The rest were by lesser-known or amateur artists."

"What did the picture look like?"

Adam wanted to know, but he also liked to look at Erin when she talked about her subject. He loved the glow of excitement on her face.

"The subject was Samuel Hall, a goldsmith. He stood before a federal mirror overhanging a fireplace. His arm was stretched along the mantle, pointing at a plain pair of silver candlesticks and a silver spoon. In front of him, calipers and a small hammer lay on an exquisite Federal table. Tools of his trade, I would think." Erin frowned and went on. "Oddly, there was also an open letter, propped up on a tiny easel. I'm not sure what that was about. As with many of these paintings, the colors had faded somewhat, but there was lots of blue, which lasts well. It's unusual to have so much backdrop. Most of the artists used a stock background and added the current subject. This looked like a custom job to me."

"What was the subject of the sampler? Ada told me how it was made."

"The family genealogy."

"Genealogy again."

"Do you want to stay? There's pasta for dinner."

"No, thanks. I still have a lot to do. I'll see you tomorrow."

The doorbell's jangle interrupted their good-byes as a customer came in.

Adam's last chore of the day was to talk Anne into helping him. He thought she was likely back at Catherine's.

∾

The porch lights glowed, turning Catherine's house into a beacon on the otherwise dark street. Adam parked in the driveway behind Anne's rental.

"Hello, Adam," said Catherine when she answered the door. "Come in."

As they walked down the hall towards the kitchen, she asked if he would like to stay for dinner.

"No thanks, although it does smell tempting. I have to ask Anne for a favor."

"A favor?" Anne smiled as she put plates and cutlery on the table. "Not to do with your job, I trust."

"Actually, yes. I need your genealogical knowledge. It's about the paintings that were stolen from the library."

Anne and Catherine exchanged puzzled glances. Clearly, the town gossip system had passed them by this time.

"What paintings?" Anne said.

"The portrait of Samuel Hall and the sampler."

"Those were the ones that I didn't see. Were they stolen here?"

"Yes. We think so. Dummy boxes were sent to Brownsville. When they opened the boxes in Brownsville, they found blank canvases in old frames."

"So they were stolen here, substituted en route, or stolen there, and the dummies put in their place."

"Looks like those are the choices."

"Where does genealogy come into it, except for the subject of the sampler?"

Adam told them James Trevelyan's story. "To get a look at those papers, to understand them, and decide if the paintings could be his, I need your help."

Anne sat and stared at Adam for a few moments. Not again, she thought. What if it happened again, and she got drawn in?

"Only the papers? Nothing else?"

"Of course."

"All right. I'll come in tomorrow. About what time?"

"Ten. Thanks, Anne."

When Adam had left, Catherine shook her head slowly at Anne.

"You should have said no. He could find help somewhere else."

"I'll spend a day, and it won't be dangerous this time."

Chapter Four

The mid-morning gossip session was in full voice when Anne stopped by Lil's on her way to the station. She outmanoeuvred a pin-striped businessman and a yellow-jacketed electrical worker for a stool at the counter.

"Hi, Peg," she said, as she grinned triumphantly at the sandy-haired woman behind the counter.

Peg's face had filled out a little, but the elegant cheekbones she shared with her Beauchamp relatives still defined her attractive face.

"I need coffees for Adam and his crew at the station."

"You passing the time of day with them?"

"A little genealogy research."

"Don't let them take up all your vacation time."

Peg gave Anne the tray of cups and a bag of creamers and sugar packets.

"I won't. See you later."

Near the door, Anne nodded to Nancy Webb, the librarian, whom she had met and disliked. She crossed the square to the steps of the courthouse.

Climbing those stairs again was harder than Anne had imagined.

She felt a little dizzy at the sight of the pockmarks the bullets made in the wall, bullets that came uncomfortably close to her head. Telling herself to get a grip, she pushed open the door.

The squad room was quiet. Brad hunched over a keyboard at the centre desk.

"Hey, Dr McPhail, how are you?" he said when he spotted her across the room.

"Great, Brad. Can you take these?"

Anne smiled up at him. He worked with her last year, and she knew him to be a coffee fiend.

"Thanks. Did you want to see Adam? He's in the office, but he has someone with him."

"I think I'm supposed to join them."

Anne peered at Adam's office, but the blinds were closed.

"I'll tell him you're here."

Adam's corner office overlooked the street on one side and, through a window, the squad room on the other. Even the door had a window in it. The first change Adam made when he received his promotion was to install blinds. A recycled desk, stacked with papers and files, and hard-backed chairs shared the only complete wall with a cabinet. Framed diplomas, hanging behind and a picture of Erin on it made the space a little more personal, but not by much. Brad held the door open for her.

"Morning, Anne. I'd like you to meet James Trevelyan."

The old man's craggy face, heavy plaid shirt, and green work pants held up by red suspenders reminded Anne unexpectedly of her long-dead father. She held out her hand, controlling the tears that threatened.

"I'm Anne McPhail. I hope I can be of some use to you, Mr. Trevelyan."

Suspicion clouded his faded grey eyes as he reluctantly shook her hand.

"Huh. This young fella thinks those pictures didn't belong to me because some old woman told him my family died out. It didn't. Here I am."

"We'll prove them wrong. Could you show me what you have so far?"

He handed the file folder over. Anne expected a chaotic jumble, from Adam's description, but the folder was organized and tidy.

He had an almost complete genealogical record, Anne decided. Documentation on his line included birth and death certificates back to Samuel Hall Leclerc in 1849. Anne's job was to find the link back to Samuel Hall and his portrait. The will that left Samuel's possessions and his house to his sister seemed genuine.

Anne leaned back in the unyielding wooden chair.

" Mr Trevelyan, I know some sources of information here in town that might help you. Do you want me to give you a list or do you want me to look at them and get back to you?"

"Do you have to take my stuff?"

What an anxious man, Anne thought. Aloud she reassured him. "No."

"Then you do it. But tell me first, not this cop."

Trevelyan stared defiantly at Adam.

"What about it, Adam? You asked me to do this."

The room became quiet with confrontation.

"The genealogy stuff, sure. If you stumble across anything about either of these crimes, it's mine."

"Mr Trevelyan?"

"All I want is the family tree and my property."

Anne accepted that as a yes as Adam nodded. Abruptly the old man stood and shook both their hands.

"Thanks."

He turned and limped toward the door, leaning heavily on his cane. He left the door open.

Anne rapidly filled a yellow legal pad with her neat but illegible handwriting. She sketched an outline of a family tree from James to his great-grandmother Mildred Hall Leclerc and her father, Samuel Hall Leclerc.

"You remembered all those names and dates, Anne? How?"

"Practice. Often patients are nervous about you writing down the more sensitive parts of the history, so I learned to remember long enough to get it on paper when they left."

"What now?"

"I think I'll begin over at the Catholic Church. In the will, Samuel Hall forgives his sister for converting to Catholicism. The church has wonderful records, and the priest is pleasant and accommodating."

∼

Adam called to Brad from his office door.

"Get the board, Brad."

Adam started a line on the story board they used to keep track of investigations, with the dead man's name and picture at the top. He added a sidebar for Trevelyan.

"What next?" asked Pete who had come in.

"You make the rounds of the bars and motels. Brad, you check the security system at the library."

"What about you?"

"I'm going to Brownsville."

Adam's route to Brownsville took him a hundred miles southeast into the Green Mountains. Mist shrouded the hills, muting the colours to mystic greys and blue-greens. The road wound upward in lazy curves, each bringing another throat-catching view. Azure pools filled in the scars on the land left by mining operations. At the lookout, Adam stopped to stand at the railing and enjoy the town, spread out on a grid below.

Church spires punctuated the streets. The mountains surrounded and so overwhelmed it that the town appeared to be one of those miniature villages set up in year-round Christmas stores.

The road spiralled into the town and followed the curve of the lakefront. In the nineteenth-century, the town was the centre of a granite-quarrying area, which supplied much of the stone for important public buildings in the state. Brownsville's quarrying history left it with a reputation as a tough and dangerous town then and now. Adam had been there on several investigations in the past, mostly into a seedy area of deteriorating company houses, not the genteel centre with its stone mansions on tree-lined streets.

Adam's destination was another Carnegie library. How many of these libraries did Andrew Carnegie build, he wondered? Anne would likely know.

This one was octagonal, raised on a cut-stone foundation. Inside the heavy oak door, six steps led up to the main floor. The children's library was to the right, adults to the left, and the art gallery downstairs. The chief librarian doubled as the curator of the art gallery.

An elderly woman stood behind the desk, stamping library cards. No computer or scanner here yet.

"Could I speak with Mr Abbott?" Adam asked, showing his police identification.

"He's down in the gallery, back through the doors and downstairs."

Adam took the stairs, followed by the clerk's curious gaze. The art gallery revealed itself as a long, windowless room, painted the shade of flat white curators in the sixties used to focus attention on the paintings and not the walls. Now it was more likely to be fuchsia or bright orange. The travelling show was still here, Adam thought, looking at the portraits hung on the walls.

The door to an office to the left of the stairs was standing open. Adam knocked on the door frame.

"Good morning," he said, showing his badge again, this time to a man standing behind his desk. "I'm Lieutenant Davidson, Culver's Mills police. I called earlier?"

The other man was about thirty-five, with a muscular upper body. No fat anywhere. As for the rest: dark slicked hair, ears tight to the head but too big for it, dark eyes behind small, square, wire-rimmed glasses. Wound tight, he thought. Odd for a librarian, but what did he know? Maybe their lives were full of stress and drama. The stark furnishings of the room reflected the man, over-tidy, nothing personal to be seen.

"Dan Abbott," the man said, putting out a hand that went with the small head. "What can I do for you?"

"You reported the theft of two paintings from the shipment you got from Culver's Mills. I need to see whatever you have lef— cartons, seals. I see you've hung the show. Why did you go on unwrapping when you found the empty boxes?"

"Because I came to them last, of course. I called the police as soon as I found the first empty box. The other pictures had to be hung for the opening of the show."

Adam went on with his questions, ignoring the lengthy explanation.

"Where did you unwrap?"

"In the central gallery. It's the only space we have. I put the wrappers in the alcove. They were identical."

The sweat glistened on his forehead and rivulets ran down either side of his face.

Nervous, Adam thought. He wondered if this was usual for him or just when talking to one of the police, or was he hiding something.

"Let me see what you have left."

The crates, not boxes, were sturdy, lined with bubble wrap. The seals on each had been neatly sliced. Adam listened while the curator babbled on, repeating his assurances the boxes were intact when they reached him. Now sweat was starting to bead on his upper lip. They walked back to the office and sat.

"Mr Abbott, what is your opinion on the value of the missing goods?"

"Goods. I'm not a dealer or a shopkeeper, sir. The value is not my business."

"Come on, Mr Abbott. You have to insure the stuff, and I'm sure you must read the trade journals."

"The most I've ever read about a Belknap earning was in a report of an auction at Skinner's in Boston in 1995. A double portrait of children sold for about one hundred and seventy thousand dollars. The subject in the picture we were to receive was not so appealing. The sampler, on the other hand, was extremely fine, at eight to ten thousand. Together I think one hundred thousand would have been reasonable."

"You seem to know a lot after all. Have you seen the pieces?"

"No, never."

"What would a thief do with them?"

"I have no idea, Lieutenant. I suppose there is a black market, but I know nothing about that."

"Will your insurance pay the loss?"

"Certainly not. They were not stolen here. The security at Culver's Mills must be poor. Their insurance should have to pay."

"We don't know where the theft occurred, Mr Abbott," Adam said as he stood up to leave. "We'll let you know."

At the door to the stairs, Adam glanced back. The librarian had reached for his phone.

Chapter Five

The walk to the Catholic Church took Anne to the river and across the bridge. The water beneath tumbled and frothed its way over the weir. Above the dam, the expanse of the millpond reflected a neighborhood of large brick homes intermixed with some smaller houses. Renovations were resurrecting some of the fine old homes, turning them back into the single-family dwellings they once were.

St. Mary's, itself a very old church, had received a face-lift with new roofing, new fencing (or at least paint on the old iron pickets), pointing of the brick and other necessary repairs. No improvement to the age-blackened oak door, she noted with relief. The church office, she remembered, was at the back, past the altar and through another oak door that was carved and pierced to match the paneling across the front of the church. Beyond the door, it was part workaday world and part ritual. The large office used by the priest for signing the register with wedding parties was to the right and beyond it the secretary's room.

Ann knocked at the door.

"Come in."

An elderly red-haired woman with a cheerful round face sat behind the desk. Her green eyes and pale, freckled skin suggested Irish ancestry to Anne, and indeed, the lady introduced herself as Marg Kennedy.

"Miss, dear, not that awful Ms. that always reminds me of an angry mosquito. What can I do for you?"

"I was hoping that Father O'Brien would be here. He was very kind to me on my last visit."

"No, dear, I'm afraid he isn't here. The poor old soul went to Burlington for a hip replacement. Won't be home till Saturday. Perhaps I could do something if it's not spiritual help you need."

"It's about genealogy. Last time I visited, Father O'Brien allowed me to work in your archive."

"Archive. Now that's a grand name for a little room. Certainly. Come along with me."

Since her last visit, Anne noticed, a computer had been added, and a neat box of computer disks replaced a wall of files. All the old registers lay flat on Mylar-covered shelves.

"What years would you like to see, dear?"

"1800 to 1850. I'm interested in baptisms at that time." Anne was hoping to hear that those years were on the computer but no such luck. Mrs Kennedy showed her the registers for 1800 to 1840 She handed one to Anne.

"This one takes in 1810-1812. Do you want to start with the earliest registers or do you want to take a lucky dip?"

"I think I'll go for the lucky dip.

Anne smiled, as she took the leather-bound volume. Miss Kennedy handed her white gloves used to protect the old paper from the acids and oils found on the skin.

"I'll leave you, dear. Call me if you need to use the computer."

"Thanks."

Anne caressed the cracked, age-softened leather once before putting on the gloves and gingerly turning fragile pages. She found the entries for 1812, but not Thomas. She started back at 1800 in the first register and reached 1812 again when Miss Kennedy knocked at the door.

"It's noon, Dr McPhail. Do you want to stay over lunch? I'm going home now."

"Could I? Do you want me to lock up for you?"

"Turn the lock and pull the door to."

"Thanks so much."

"Oh, you're very welcome. I hope you find those old folk."

Half an hour later, Anne found him. The handwriting in the register changed, and in the elegant copperplate of the new priest she read Thomas Leclerc, infant son of Charity Hall and Alexander Leclerc, born June 1, 1814, baptized Sept. 18, 1814.

Now she had Thomas Leclerc, son of Samuel's sister Charity, according to the old man. She needed to go further back, to find the link between Charity, Samuel and Thomas. A marriage record of Alexandre and Charity, which should be at St. Mary's and a baptism for Charity and Samuel which should be... where? Anne knew that there was an Episcopal church. Perhaps she would find it there. In the meantime, she was going back to Catherine's for lunch and to make a phone call.

As they ate in Catherine's kitchen, Anne told Catherine about her morning at the police station and the church.

"It looks like the church came into some money. New roof, new paint on the fence and a computer system in the archive."

"People are always leaving money to the Catholic Church. Father O'Brien works hard for his for parishioners."

"Not some of the blackmail money?"

Anne referred to the case in which she had been involved, as she reached for her half of the stuffed croissant they were sharing for lunch.

"No. Everything went back, as far as I know, to the people that were victims of that horrible woman. Would you like some soup?"

"No thanks."

"What are you doing this afternoon?"

"Calling Thomas."

Anne put down her sandwich and watched the birds at the feeder.

"Are you still seeing him in Toronto?" Catherine asked after a few moments.

"Yes, I am, but I'm not sure where we're going with this."

"Does it have to go somewhere? Are you eager to get married again?"

"Not really, so perhaps you're right, and I should see what happens."

After they cleared up, Anne left a message at the Beauchamp home for Thomas and worked on her genealogy files. She was making herself tea when the phone rang.

"Anne."

"Hi, Thomas."

"I wonder if you would come out to dinner with my mother and my daughter?" he asked.

"I'd be delighted."

Catherine looked a question at her from across the kitchen.

"Dinner with his mother and one of his daughters."

"The girls will be harder than the boy. Girls don't accept a new woman very well."

"I'm going to dinner, not marrying the man."

"I'm just saying."

Anne drove out to the old stone house. With its deep-set windows and bright blue door, it was one of Anne's favorites among the homes in Culver's Mills. A young woman in a maid's uniform answered the door and welcomed Anne.

"Mrs Beauchamp is in the sitting room, Doctor," she said when Anne introduced herself. "Please follow me."

The decorating of the house showed two hands at work, or maybe three. The architecture had been opened up, and the walls painted light colors, but the furniture comprised American antiques of the eighteenth and early nineteenth centuries. Those were Mrs Beauchamp's taste, Anne knew. On the other hand, the art was solidly twentieth-century, some representational, some not. Anne's favorite was a Canadian painting, from one of the Beaver Hall group of women painters from Montreal. Thomas, she suspected, or perhaps Claire, his art student daughter.

"Anne, how lovely to see you again."

Mrs. Beauchamp's stately figure rose from her straight-backed armchair. She kissed Anne and gestured her to a companion chair on the other side of the fireplace.

"Thomas is a bit delayed, but I expect him in a few minutes. Tell me what you have been doing since we last met."

Anne took a barge trip in France, and they talked about her experiences until they heard the front door open and Thomas's deep voice greet the maid.

Thomas Beauchamp, heir to the Beauchamp fortune, business-man, and world-class skier as a young man was a lithe and tanned fifty, with his mother's black eyes and prominent nose. He bent over to kiss his mother and then embraced Anne. His dark eyes smiled into hers.

"It's so good to see you again, but what's this I hear about you finding a body?"

"A body." his mother said. "Not again, Anne?"

"I'm afraid so."

She told them about finding the body and what Adam asked her to do.

"Try to stay out of trouble this time," Thomas said.

"Oh, there isn't any danger. It's research."

At that their dinner was announced as Claire came in and the conversation turned elsewhere.

Chapter Six

Pete took the quick left to Commerce Road. A run-down motel sat at the end of a street of warehouses and factories. You had to know it was here, he thought. Maybe someone local put Andrews onto it if he stayed here.

Two cars were parked in front, one by the manager's office, the other further along at unit three unit. A red-tiled roof gave the place its name—Red Roof Inn. A rusting eavestrough clung to the roof line. Below, tobacco-brown stains marked the white stucco exterior.

Six units: three up, three down. Black paint peeled from the railings along the stairs and outside corridor. A row of vending machines with the usual—chips, pop, chocolate bars—marked the manager's office; an afterthought tacked on to the end of the row. A short man with brown skin and black hair huddled over a computer at a desk in the corner of the office. No one was at the counter.

"May I help you?"

His accent suggested Indian or Pakistani to Pete.

"Have you seen this guy here?" Pete asked, showing him the DMV picture of the dead man.

The manager was eager to help, identifying the picture of the dead man as the occupant of unit six, upstairs from three. He checked in three, four days ago. The manager hadn't seen him since, so he said. The car in front of three, a late model Ford Taurus, was his rental. It was locked and empty. The motel room was empty too if you didn't count beer cans, pizza boxes and dirty clothes. No signs of a struggle but a bloody mess covered the pillow. What looked to be bone fragments and brains and blood spattered the wall beyond. The manager was at his elbow, gagging.

"Get out if you're going to heave."

The little man stumbled from the room, hit the railing, and threw up. Nice for anyone below, Pete thought.

He spoke into his shoulder radio, calling for a forensics crew and backup. Now he knew why the guy was naked. Killed here and moved to Catherine's backyard.

When Adam arrived, Pete stood alone in front of the rental car. The forensics team had nothing beyond the brains and blood to report, so far.

"Have you searched the car yet?" Adam asked Pete.

"It's next. They've done the handles and window, driver's side."

"Pop the trunk."

Blood smeared the carpet of the trunk; otherwise, it was empty.

"He was carried in it a while after he died, boss."

"Looking for a place to dump him. Ask around Catherine's neighborhood. Maybe someone saw the car. Did the motel owner notice anyone else here?"

"No."

"Tried the other units?"

"Not yet."

"I'm going back to the station if you need me. Where's Brad?"

"He went to the library, but he should have finished there."

At the library, Brad checked the high-end security system. Any disruption triggered the alarm and called the monitoring service. Either it wasn't turned on, or someone had the code.

Nancy Webb was in her office when he knocked. Her face and voice said "not again".

"Ms. Webb, who has the code for your security system?"

"I do, as well as Madeline Fox, Ada Warren and the installer. Oh yes, and that teenager, Chrissy. Why Ada gave her the code, I will never understand. I have a strict rule about who does what around here and if she followed it, we wouldn't be in this trouble."

A lot of talk for Nancy, Brad thought. Trying to blame the kid.

"Do you have addresses for Ms. Fox and the name and address of the installer?"

"Yes. What about Chrissy?"

"I know where she lives."

"I'm sure she didn't turn on the system."

"Thanks for your time, Ms. Webb."

When Adam walked through the door into the squad room, Brad slammed a phone into the receiver.

"Take it easy on the equipment, Brad. What's up?"

"I'm searching for the people who have access to the code at the library. The installer is out of business; Mrs. Fox is out of town; Mrs. Warren says herself and Chrissy, and Chrissy's dad hung up on me."

"Let's go see him."

All small towns have a fringe of poor, rundown properties, Adam supposed, sometimes inside town limits, sometimes not. Bassett's property was the shabbiest on the dirt road that led past his home. A battered sign, proclaiming BASSETT & Sons Body Shop, decorated a Quonset hut at the back. Derelict old cars, truck caps and engine parts littered the yard around the shop and the house. The cab of the semi Bassett drove filled the lane. Somewhere out behind the house a dog howled steadily.

Bassett was Chrissy Chambers's stepfather, and they heard him before they saw him. The screen door burst open as they approached the house. A young girl hurled herself down the steps calling over her shoulder, "...and I'm never coming back."

"Good riddance, bitch," came the answering roar as Chrissy careered into Adam.

"Slow down, Chrissy. What's going on?"

Her voice choked with sobs, she raged at Adam.

"He's drunk again. Beating up my mom, again. I'm leaving. Mrs. Warren said I can come to her and I'm going. He won't let me have my clothes, and I paid for them. He won't pay for anything for me. All he cares about are 'his boys'."

"I'll get your clothes, Chrissy and then I'll take you to Ada's," Adam said.

"You're not coming in here, cop."

Bassett stood on the doorstep, cradling a shotgun.

"What you want to wave that around for, Gord? The kid needs her clothes. Where's her mother?"

"You never mind about her mother."

"If I don't see her, I'm going to assume she's hurt and come in there."

A pale, gaunt woman appeared behind Bassett as he lowered the shotgun. Even at a distance, Adam could see a developing bruise on her right cheek and the bruises on her wrists.

"Do you want to come with me, Mrs. Bassett?"

"No, I'll stay here. I'll be all right. I'll get Chrissy's clothes."

She reappeared moments later carrying a black plastic garbage bag. She edged past her husband and stumbled down the steps to Brad.

"Bassett, if she shows up at an Emergency Room, or worse, I'll be back for you."

"We'll take Chrissy to Ada's and talk to her there," he said as he swung into the passenger side.

"How ya doing, Chrissy?"

"I'm okay."

The fragrance of chicken soup met them at Ada's door. Ada took one look, enveloped Chrissy in her arms and led her into the kitchen. Adam and Brad followed. Soon the trembling girl, wrapped in one of Ada's was sitting at the pine table, hunched over a bowl of soup.

"I can't eat, Mrs. Warren," she said as she put the spoon down.

"Try a little, to help take away the shock."

Chrissy took a tentative sip and another. Adam watched until he saw her color return along with her appetite and then filled Ada in on what happened.

"I have the code, and I gave it to Chrissy so she could lock up. Chrissy, did you give that code to anyone?" Ada said.

"No. I kept it in my agenda, in my backpack. I never talked about it or gave it to anyone."

"Did anyone in your family know?"

"I guess he did, because he picked me up when I closed up, but I didn't tell him where it was."

Chrissy's bravado slipped, and tears ran down her cheeks.

"Do you think anyone in your family could have gone through your backpack?"

"Yes," she mumbled, her head buried in Mrs. Warren's shoulder.

"Isn't this enough for now?" Ada asked, looking at Adam.

"Sure. If she remembers anything specific, call me. Don't let her go out and don't let that guy in here."

As they drove to the station, Adam told Brad to check Bassett's record and to compare his prints to any they found on the security system or the boxes in Brownsville.

Chapter Seven

The next day was cold, with a faint promise of snow. Anne walked the few blocks to the Episcopal Church. The white clapboard building, set back in a graveyard, looked as though it could have used an anonymous donor or two. A sign at the front announced its minister as David Dodds and the church as All Souls.

A white-painted, badly-used door at the back of the church bore a small sign: Church Office. Thin described the man behind the desk, Anne thought. Thin body, thin moustache, even his tiny, capped teeth were set in a narrow jaw.

A deep, irritated voice asked, "Yes?"

"I'm looking for Mr. Dodds."

"I am Pastor Dodds."

Anne wondered what irritated him? An arduous passage in a sermon, perhaps.

"I'm Dr. Anne McPhail," she said in her formal, at-the-office, voice. "I wonder if you have any parish record books. I'm doing some genealogical research."

"I don't have time to help you."

He dropped his gaze and leafed through papers on his desk.

"I don't need any help but access to your books. I'm helping the police with an investigation—the theft at the library?"

Her voice trailed off, as he paused long enough to look up at her again.

"Fine, fine. The records are in the back."

He pointed to a door to the right of his desk.

The tiny windowless room, unventilated in any way, reeked of must and fungus. The registers stood on end on a white painted shelf.

Anne jumped as the minister came up behind her and said, "Perhaps you'd like to work at my desk. I'll be out for a while, and it's dark in here."

Anne supposed she misjudged the man. Not the first time that happened. She made up her mind about people too fast and often regretted her first opinion.

"Thank you. I would."

Hunting through the registers, Anne found volumes from the late 1700s and another from the late 1840s. Time passed, and Anne's nose, sensitive always, started to warn of impending allergic attack. As she sneezed and dripped, she found, written in a tiny, crabbed hand, the baptismal record for Charity, infant daughter of Thomas Hall and Amy Ridout Hall, born August 9, 1794, and baptized Nov. 10, 1794. Where was Samuel?

Assuming he was older, Anne turned the stained and fragmented pages back. By now her eyes were red, and her nose ran. These pages are dying, she thought. Soon there will be no records left.

Many records from the 1790s were lost or illegible, but she found Samuel, born May 15, 1790, baptized May 30.

Now that she had Charity and Samuel, all she needed was evidence Thomas married in this church.

But nothing. No Thomas in 1847 or 1848 or 1849. If he married Rebecca Simpson, he hadn't done it here.

Simpson, she thought. Simpson was an Ulster name, or Scottish. She wondered if there was a Presbyterian Church in Culver's Mills.

She replaced the books and was washing her hands in the tiny wash-room when the minister returned.

"I suppose they are a little dusty," he said.

"They'll be gone soon."

"What?"

"Paper and leather deteriorate. Your storeroom is the worst possible place for any old book. Couldn't you ask an archive or even the Catholic Church to hold them for you? St. Mary's has a climate-controlled room with lots of space."

"Certainly not. What are you thinking?"

"I'm thinking that unless you get them into a better environ-ment, they'll be gone."

Anne picked up her briefcase and put out her hand. "Thank you for letting me see them."

"You think they're that bad?"

"Yes. I'm so sorry to have to tell you this," she said a little more gently. "Speak to the priest. He's very helpful."

"I will, and I'll take the matter up with my board. Is there anything more I can do for you?"

"Could you tell me if there's a Presbyterian Church here?"

"Yes. The Auld Kirk, on Reston Street, but I don't know if they kept their registers."

"If they're Scots Presbyterian, they did."

She shook the minister's hand and walked to the Auld Kirk.

She was lucky in her hunt. By the time she finished at the church she had all the information she had needed. She completed the genealogy, and old Trevelyan was right. He was a direct descendant of the original owner or rather inheritor of the painting. Whether or not that meant he had any right to it and the rest of property, Anne didn't know. If each person who had owned the house, bought it in good faith, it would be hard to sort out. A case for the courts, she supposed. On the other hand, if the painting were hidden in that house all this time perhaps it would be different. Not her problem, Anne thought. She would drive out to his place and tell him.

Before going, she recorded it all on her computer and copied it to a jump drive. She didn't want to lose all the information after so much work.

She thought about Trevelyan on the way to the house. Sometimes the elderly did develop obsessions like this with a property. It poisoned a life. Trevelyan didn't need it, from what Adam said about the place in the country. She finished the drive through the sugarbush at Trevelyan's mailbox. Odd, she thought, the gates of the property were open. Adam mentioned the security here.

A black truck, formidable in the narrow space, partially blocked the end of the lane near the house. Anne parked beside it. When she got out, she saw a crumpled form between the house and the truck.

She knew before she got to him that it was Trevelyan, still in his plaid shirt and suspenders. He lay face down; dirt filled his nose. She cleared that away, felt for a pulse and pressed her fingers into the pale skin of his forearm. The long seconds before the blood returned, the weak pulse that fluttered at his wrist, and his clammy gray skin suggested an ominously low blood pressure. Blood oozed around a gaping hole in the back of his shirt.

She took her cell from her pocket and jammed it back in. No bars, no service. She hoped there was a phone in the house as she ran into the front room. Nothing. Maybe in the kitchen. A black, old-fashioned dial-phone hung on the wall. Anne's voice was shaking as she dialed 911.

"What service?"

"Police and ambulance. A man's been shot. He's dying."

"Where are you?"

"The Trevelyan property on Sugar Bush Road. I don't know the number."

"Stay on the phone."

"I can't. I have to go back to him. Hurry."

Anne ran back to the old man, tearing off her coat to cover him, and, using a towel that she grabbed in the kitchen, put pressure on the wound. His pulse was a faint thrill under her fingers, becoming more irregular as his respirations changed to feeble gasps. He's going, she thought. They won't be in time.

Who did this? Where was the owner of the truck in the lane? Was he still here?

Too late, she heard footsteps behind her, looked back, then nothing.

Chapter Eight

The paramedics worked quickly—intravenous lines in, the woman strapped to a backboard, both patients hooked to monitors. They intubated the man, bagged him and gave him drugs. A second ambulance arrived; the first left with the woman.

Adam arrived with the next cruiser.

"How is he?"

"Touch and go. We're taking him now."

"Where?"

"Culver's."

"His name is James Trevelyan. He's about seventy, and he has a bad chest, asthma or something."

"Thanks, Lieutenant."

"Who's the woman?"

"Don't know. The car's over there."

Adam whispered, "Oh, no."

"Pardon, Lieutenant."

"Her name's Anne McPhail. She's a doctor, about forty. Good health."

Adam's face was white as he stood, turning his hat over and over in his hands. His inner thoughts were mostly profane and guilt-ridden.

"How bad was she?"

"The other crew had her."

The ambulance left as the Sheriff's van arrived. Sheriff Bill Perkins' burly figure emerged. A longtime friend of Adam's, he pumped Adam's hand.

"What's the story?"

"You know about the murder in Culver's, and the theft from the art gallery?"

"Yeah?"

"The man who lives here, James Trevelyan, claims he's the rightful heir of two of the pictures. The woman is Anne McPhail —you remember—the Canadian doctor who helped us last year in the Russian case. She did some research for Trevelyan. I asked her to. Goddamit, why didn't she call me before she came out here?"

"Would you have told her not to come?"

"Probably not. No, I didn't think there was any risk in what she was doing."

They turned to the scene. One of the men bagged a shotgun. A patch of blonde hair mixed with blood adhered to the stock.

Adam searched the ransacked farmhouse for the old man's information on his family. He found most of it amongst the papers strewn across the floor and dining room table, even the will. Nothing about the painting. What the hell was so valuable they shot Trevelyan? Shot with his own gun judging from the empty hooks above the mantle.

Adam left the scene to Perkins and drove back to town and the hospital. A two-story, red-brick structure built around an atrium replaced the Victorian mansion plus additions that served the town up until two years before. Pete met him outside the door to Anne's second-floor room.

"Anne's not here. They took her down for an MRI."

"How is she?"

"They say okay, doing as well as can be expected. You know how they talk."

"What about Trevelyan?"

"Not so good. He's in surgery. The doc said his chest is bad. Did you find anything at the scene?"

"Not so far."

Adam turned when the elevator doors open. Anne's eyes were closed, but she didn't have any tubes, he saw with relief, except for the one in the nose most trauma patients had and an intravenous.

"Can I come in?"

"Sure," the nurse replied, "for a few minutes."

"Adam?"

"Yes. Wait until you're in your bed."

Adam looked a question at the nurse.

"She's okay. No fractures and no hemorrhage. A concussion, the doctor said. She'll drift in and out for a while, though."

"Can I talk to her?"

"For a little while. She's still pretty much out of it."

"Okay."

Adam sat by the bed and took Anne's hand, still and white on the blanket.

"Anne?"

"Mmm. Adam."

"Are you awake?"

"A little. What happened to me?"

"Someone hit you."

"Hit me."

Then she remembered.

"Trevelyan, is he dead?"

"No, in surgery. Did you see anyone?"

"No."

"Why did you go there?"

"Finished. Wanted to tell him he was right."

Anne forced the words out past her dry lips.

"Did you take your results to him?"

"Yes, in my car."

"Okay, you rest. We'll talk later."

When Adam came out of Anne's room, he faced the long counter of the nurse's station. He spoke to the red-headed charge nurse.

"I'll leave an officer outside the door. I don't believe whoever did this will try again, but report strangers to him, will you?"

"Yes, I will."

A bell rang as the elevator door opened. Adam looked over to see Thomas Beauchamp striding towards him, red-faced and curling his hands into tight fists.

"Davidson, what do you think you are doing, using innocent women to do your police work? This is the third time she's been hurt working for you, and I won't stand for it."

"Come in here," Adam said, pointing to a room to the side the doctors used for talking to families. Thomas followed him in.

"Look, you're worried about her. So am I, but I have a murder to solve, and Anne has the knowledge to help me. She knows the risks, and she accepts them. Unfortunately, she decided to go out to Trevelyan's without talking to me."

"You didn't send her out there?"

"No, I didn't, and I wouldn't have."

Thomas sat down abruptly and put his head in his hands. "How is she?"

"She'll be okay. Do you want to go in to see her? I'll tell them it's okay."

"In a few minutes."

Pete called in his younger brother Dave, who was on the door when Adam left.

"Check all the name tags, Dave. Make sure the faces match."

"Most of the doctors don't wear them."

"Check them with the nurses."

"Will do."

Thomas paced outside of Anne's room, waiting for the nurse to finish her 'neuro-vitals', whatever they were. The young policeman stood at the door, eyeing the traffic in the hallway. When the nurse left the room, the policeman motioned him in.

Anne drifted back to sleep. Thomas sat beside her bed, resisting the temptation to take her hand. A few minutes later her body jerked, and her terrified eyes opened, staring at him without recognition for a moment.

"Thomas, I was dreaming."

"Go back to sleep. You're safe now, dear heart," he said.

"I keep dreaming about footsteps behind me and a smell that is pleasant and frightening all at the same time."

What seemed like moments later, she awoke to find her room dark and Thomas sitting at her bedside.

"Thomas, how long have you been here? How long have I been asleep?" she croaked, her voice thick with sleep.

Thomas took her hand.

"An hour. How are you?"

"Better. Was Adam here? I dreamed I heard him fighting with you."

"We had a few words."

"Why?"

"Why? Because this is the third time you have been almost killed working for that guy, and I won't stand for it."

Thomas voice and temper rose again.

"Thomas, it's my business, my risk, not yours."

"I made it my business. For God's sake, you're a pediatrician, not some kind of private detective."

"It was my fault. I went out there without telling anyone because I had promised the old man I would give him my findings first. But I don't owe you an explanation or need your permission to get on with my life."

At that moment, the nurse came in, apparently oblivious to the tension in the room.

"I have to take your vitals again, Anne," she said. "I wonder if your visitor could leave for a few minutes."

"Of course."

Thomas said a perfunctory good-bye to Anne and left.

"Are you feeling all right? You're flushed, and your heart rate is much higher."

"It's not my concussion. Just men."

"I thought there was some tension in here."

"I'm too tired to worry right now," Anne said as she closed her eyes again.

As Adam drove away from the hospital a phone call from Bill Perkins told him they were towing Anne's car to the Culver's Mills impound lot. Bill had a question.

"How valuable are those paintings?"

"Hundred thousand, maybe. Give or take. Maybe much less."

"Sounds like more than a hundred grand worth of trouble."

"Yes, it does."

An orange and violet sunset stained the window at Lil's as Adam parked in front. The solitary customer was having a quiet meal at a window table.

"Hi, Adam," said Peg. "Usual?"

"Evening, Peg. Yes, but make it two sandwiches. I haven't eaten all day."

"Sure."

Adam sat at the counter and tucked into his favorite chicken salad and fries. Peg had added a side salad in an attempt to improve his nutrition. When he finished, he saw that the other customer hadn't left.

"Who's the lady in the corner? She looks familiar."

"Madeline Fox."

"Oh, yes."

Adam recalled that Madeline Fox was the curator or director of the art gallery. She had been out of town when the paintings went missing. When he finished his dinner, he went over to her table.

"Ms. Fox, I'm Lieutenant Davidson, Culver police. Could I have a word with you?"

"Of course," she said, folding her newspaper. "I've wanted to talk to you. Have you made any progress in finding the painting and sampler?"

"Not so far. I wonder if you could describe them to me." Mrs. Fox's round face crumpled into a charming smile. "Oh, yes. I studied them quite carefully as I'm going to write a small paper on the show."

Adam smiled at her enthusiastic voice as she went on.

"The painting was a three-quarter length study of a gentleman. Quite attractive and well dressed. He had rings on two fingers—a small signet ring on the fifth finger of his right hand, and a ring with a large red stone, likely a garnet, on his left hand, on the fourth finger. He was standing at a mantelpiece with his hand and arm outstretched along it with the index finger pointing at some silver pieces on the mantle. These were a tankard and a candlestick. Gold-smith tools, something that looked like an ingot of gold, and a bar of silver lay on the table beside him. A paper was propped on an easel. All in all, it is the portrait of a wealthy and successful man. Quite elaborate for Belknap, I might add.

"And the sampler?"

"It was not precisely a sampler, although the owner called it that. The artist used many stitch patterns on it but was not done as a showpiece for the stitching craft but rather as a memorial or genealogical record. It was quite lovely in silks and gold thread as well as many other colors. A tree stood in the center with names and dates of family members embroidered on the branches. One man stood beside one of the trunks of the tree—it had three—with one hand pointing down as if to say This is our land. We are planted here. The house behind looks like the one Evan's is in."

She paused for breath and was about to go on when Adam interrupted.

"What family was it?"

"Oh, the Leclercs and the Halls. Mildred Hall Leclerc made it in 1875. It is signed and dated."

"It was a record; no one would need actual genealogical records?"

"I think it isn't enough. People who do genealogical research want more sources. Do ask Anne McPhail. I hear she's in town."

"I will. Thank you, Ms. Fox. Do you know anything about the show and the packing up?"

"Only what should have happened."

"I have that. Thanks again."

As Adam left, he thought about the interview. No nervousness, steady, and keen on her subject. He didn't think it likely she was involved.

Sam, his feline companion, complained loudly as soon as he turned the key in the lock. He was going to have to get her a friend soon. She was a cat that liked company.

Chapter Nine

Hospitals in small towns are quiet at night. Only the emergency room was active with nurses, patients, and one or two doctors. Throughout the rest, the hall lights were dimmed. A bright light marked the room of an extremely ill patient. Nurses murmured at the nursing station.

Anne woke, heard the familiar sound of the nurses, and comforted, went back to sleep.

In a remote sub-basement, a figure emerged from a closet behind the boilers. Nothing but a computer attended the three boilers that replaced a monster of a machine and its human minders. The person paused and listened before running up the metal stairs to a panel near the exit doors. Inserting two clips, he bypassed a connection. A hospital cap on his head and a name tag clipped to his anonymous greens transformed him into a hospital worker. Close enough to fool a casual observer, he hoped.

Most of the staff used the front, unalarmed stairwells but opening the back doors triggered a buzzer to warn nurses if a confused patient tried to leave. No one was likely to question another hospital worker at that time of night.

The back stairs opened near the nursing station outside the

intensive care unit. Push buzzer for entrance read the sign on the unlocked door of the ICU. The front entrance was in full view of the nursing station of the adjoining floor. Another door opened into the hallway of an adjoining unit. A hospital security guard nodded in the chair outside the ICU's main door, and two nurses worked at the nearby nursing station.

To reach the back door, he had to walk past the nurses and the security guard. With luck, they wouldn't give him a second glance. Maybe the nurses would be tired, less vigilant at this time of night.

Luck had been with him in the stairwells, but the security guard looked at him and his badge as he walked past. Was he suspicious? He listened for a yell or following footsteps as he continued down the hallway and around the corner but nothing. He grabbed a stack of towels off a linen cart. They should be good enough to explain his presence in the ICU.

Now he was through the door. Dim under-counter lighting and the greenish glow from the cardiac monitors lit the unit. He expected more activity. He pulled up his mask.

The man in the first bed slept, unassisted by a ventilator. Not Trevelyan. The next held an elderly woman. He would have to go further into the unit and closer to the desk. A middle-aged guy, pale but still awake, stared at him.

He could feel his own heart pounding. If he didn't find Trevelyan soon, he would need a bed here himself. Three spots left. The far one was empty. A curtain obscured the one beside him. A nurse might be in there.

He could see Trevelyan next. The nurses would know if something happened to him. He would have to use the heroin and get out. He slipped into the cubicle, took a syringe out of his pocket, and started injecting.

"Hey," a nurse yelled. "Get away from that patient."

He sprinted past her, pushing her back into a cart and reached the door. He hadn't injected all the heroin. Had it been enough?

Trevelyan had seen his face. He had to die. Halfway down the stairs, the code blue sounded. Enough.

Footsteps pounded down the stairs behind him, but he ran through the door on the ground level and across the hall to the basement stairwell before the guard caught up with him. He stopped running and panted in the stairwell until his breathing returned to normal. He left some clothes in the boiler room. Why would they look down there? There was no one in the ground floor corridor. He sauntered along to the door and out and over to his car.

He was putting coins in the exit slot when the first police car turned in. Safe.

Chapter Ten

P ete's voice on the phone.

"We need you at the hospital. Someone tried to kill Trevelyan. He may not live."

Adam shook himself awake and grabbed his clothes.

The cardiac arrest team was packing up when Adam arrived. A steady rhythm pulsed across the monitor.

"Hold it a minute," he said. "Is everyone here who knows what happened?"

The charge nurse looked over at him and nodded.

"Okay. I want you to keep the outcome to yourselves. If anyone asks, shake your head. We need to let the guy think he succeeded. I'll want to talk to everyone who was here when the attempt was made. Everyone else, give your names to the officer at the desk. Do you all understand?"

Three people were from off the unit—doctors from the emergency room and a respiratory technologist. He spoke to them and satisfied himself no word would come from them.

"What will we tell admitting?"

This came from the charge nurse as she filled out the cardiac arrest record.

"Can you tell them he died?"

"Not without triggering a huge amount of paperwork."

"I'll speak to them."

Adam knew the chances of keeping Trevelyan's survival quiet were slim, but even a day of silence might be helpful.

"Who saw this guy?"

A tiny blond nurse with a noticeable bruise forming on her forehead raised her hand.

"I did before he slammed me into the cart over there."

"What did he look like? Did you recognize him?"

"No. He wore greens and a cap and mask. He had surgical gloves on too. About five nine, thin. What hair I could see was brown. His eyes were brown and scared."

"Anything else. Anything unusual?"

"He had big ears."

"What about the patients?"

The nurses looked at one another. They didn't want the patients disturbed.

"Come on, ladies. One question won't hurt."

The charge nurse said, "Mr. Babcock could have seen him."

"Let's ask. Where is he?"

The nurse took Adam into the cubicle. God, he looks bad, thought Adam.

"Dave. A policeman wants to talk to you."

Dave opened his eyes and focussed on Adam's face. "Dave, did you see a man in greens pass your door before all the noise and confusion started?"

"Yeah. Was that a man? Slight, big ears."

"Would you know him again?"

"No. He wore a mask."

He closed his eyes and drifted away.

"That's all," the nurse said.

Adam, Brad and Pete held a hurried conference in the hallway outside the ICU.

"Adam, that alarm must have been bypassed," Brad said.

"Okay. Find out where the box is and check it out."

A female deputy stood a few feet away and approached Adam when he had finished talking.

"Lieutenant, when I turned into the hospital, a car was leaving the other gate. A beige Mazda, older. I didn't catch the plates. The guy driving wore greens, but I couldn't see his face."

"Good. Thanks, Arlene."

He turned to Pete.

"He left in a hurry. He may have walked into the hospital before it locked up, in his own clothes. We need to find them. Go over the area around the alarm panel. I'm going down to check on Anne."

The nurses on Anne's ward looked up at Adam, surprised to see anyone from outside at that time of night.

"What can I do for you, Adam?" asked Jocelyn.

"Hey, Jocelyn. I'd like to look in on Dr. McPhail. We had an incident upstairs, and I need to be sure she's all right."

Jocelyn Beens was one of those unusual people who never asked more than she needed to know. She nodded and walked across the hall. Anne's quiet snoring filled the room and the nurse's flashlight illuminated her peaceful face. Jocelyn backed out through the door, closing it behind her.

"She's okay."

"Thanks. I'll be back in the morning."

Adam opened the door to his house at about the same time as a boy on the outskirts of town was waking up to go fishing.

Chapter Eleven

Eleven-year-old Jamie Corrigan was a passionate fisherman.
Since he was seven years old, his parents had given up
trying to make him go to school on opening and closing
day. Early dawn found him sitting quietly in his tin boat, trailing a
line, waiting for the last strike of the season, convinced as always it
would be the biggest. Tapper's Lake, at the end of McCord Lane,
was his favorite spot. No one bothered him. No noise to disturb the
fish, at least not usually.

Jamie kept his little boat docked in a bay that bordered his
grandfather's farm. Grass Lake, part of Tapper's but separated by
the causeway around the point. Jamie's spot lay close to the bank, in
Grass Lake, but hidden from most of it by overhanging willow
branches.

Further along the shore, a short stretch of beach allowed access
to the water. A car backed down the grassy slope. A man got out and
stood, watching the road. Jamie wondered if the man was going to
fish from the shore or the bridge.

But the man didn't seem to be planning to fish. A bigger guy
walked in from the road. They talked for a minute, and then the
first one got in the car. No, not in. Jamie squinted. The man leaned

into the car and turned on the engine, shattering the silence, sending a pair of angry geese straight up, honking their disapproval. Both men heaved on the back of the car.

It was going straight into the lake. An avid watcher of television, he knew this meant Crime. He'd better be still. Now the car hit the water. They opened all the windows, so the car slid fast under the water, with a final burst of bubbles. The two men had disappeared. An engine roared on McCord Lane. At that moment a trout struck, and all thoughts of crime and police left in the joy of the fish. It was going to be a great day.

Adam thought there wasn't much point in going to bed as he fed Sam and set out into the pale light. He ran into a mist that hung over the town at the bridge, where he stood for a moment in the cool gray haze, watching the river frothing over the weir. Scaffolding covered the face of the old mill. Renovation plans included a theatre, an art gallery, a restaurant and a meeting hall. Which gallery? Competition for the one at the library or would it be moving to the new space.

As he ran on, a car overtook him. A beige Mazda. He caught the last three numbers of the Vermont plate. 752. A break? Not so many Japanese cars in town. One dealer sold Chevies and an occasional Caddy, the other Fords, mainly trucks. If you wanted anything else, you had to travel—for some models, as far as Burlington.

Adam changed his route to take him behind Erin's building. There was a soft glow behind the windows of the second floor. They decided that if she turned the lights, on he would come up. If not, not. Erin liked her sleep.

Erin's husky, early-morning voice answered his buzz. "Come on up."

"Early run?"

She let him in, declining his sweaty offer of a hug with a laugh.

"Yeah, I was called out to the hospital."

"Is Anne all right?"

"Yes, but someone tried to kill Trevelyan. He may not make it."

Adam filled the cups from the pot and put milk into Erin's.

"What's going on?"

"I don't know yet. There may be two separate crimes, the shooting and the theft, or they may be linked. I'm assuming the attack on Trevelyan relates to the theft at the library, but whether that is connected to the murder, I don't know. The attacker at the hospital was careless and let a patient see his face. We're not releasing the fact that Trevelyan survived. What have you got on for today?"

"The usual. I'm going to the travel agent's later. Could you meet me there, about one?"

"I'll try. Gotta go."

When he turned into the parking lot late, he recognized the old pickup Ted Atkins drove. He and Ted had an uneasy relationship, half friendly, half professional. The professional side had frequent problems as Ted pushed for information Adam wasn't prepared to give him.

The reporter was gossiping with the receptionist when Adam walked through the heavy door that separated the police station from the courthouse proper.

"Hey, Adam. What's this about an attack at the hospital?"

"Come into my office. What have you heard?"

"Police action there this morning, including you called out from your beauty sleep. What gives?"

He hasn't got it, Adam thought.

"Nothing I can talk about now. Publishing anything would put at least two people in harm's way."

"Come on. Give me something."

"Sorry, but that's how it is. I'll give it to you when I think it's safe."

"To me, not to Burlington."

As always, Ted's instinct was to go for the scoop.

"Sure."

After the reporter ambled out, Adam turned to the reports on his desk. A few hours later he sat in his office, mulling the evidence so far. The search of the hospital turned up a pile of abandoned clothes and the bypassed security panel in the boiler room. The clothes were no help—unisex, gray sweats. If they found a suspect, the lab could match DNA.

The security guard, who, to be fair, had been half-asleep when the orderly walked by, saw the man's face but all he remembered was a thin, not very tall man. All over thin, face included, he said. The guard spent a long morning looking at mug books but found nothing.

The suspect wore surgical gloves, according to the nurse he pushed, so fingerprints were unlikely. The syringe left at the scene contained heroin. The doctor reversed its effects, so Trevelyan was still alive, at least for now.

The DMV search turned up a car stolen the day before in Burlington as well as six others at home with their owners. If he had any suspects, he could check their whereabouts for the time of the theft, but he didn't even have a long list of possibles, never mind a short one.

He crashed his boots to the floor and sat up when the phone rang.

"Good morning, Adam."

Anne's voice was strong and cheerful.

"Anne. You're feeling better?"

"Much. I'm at Catherine's now. I'm staying in town for a few days though. Mr. Trevelyan? Do you know why he was shot? And how is he now?"

"No, not yet."

Adam went on to tell her about the attack on Trevelyan and got a promise she and Catherine would keep it to themselves.

"Do you have a new assignment for me? I warn you I am going to ask for danger pay," she said.

"I can come over and show you a description of the stolen items if you feel up to it?"

"Sure."

~

Catherine's home needed a paint job, Adam thought as he parked in the driveway but both boys would be going to college this year. College would win over paint with Catherine every time. Otherwise, the gray white-trimmed house, set in Catherine's rambling garden, looked fine. Anne and Catherine waved from the porch.

Catherine had replaced her Adirondack chairs with white wicker, cheerful with floral patterned cushions. Adam sprawled in one of them. Catherine handed him a mug of tea.

"Do you need privacy?" Catherine asked.

"No. In fact, you may be able to help as well. None of the stolen items are that valuable. Maybe there's no connection between the body and the art gallery."

"I think there is. Remember the bit of pasteboard you showed to me?" Anne said.

"Sure."

"I knew I had seen that somewhere and yesterday, I remembered. Apparently, it took a blow to the head. It was a ticket to the show at the library."

"There were tickets?"

"Yes, to provide a head count."

"Strange thing for him to hold onto unless he saw it coming and wanted to tell us something."

"Did you connect him with any local people?"

Catherine put a tray down on the glass-topped wicker table in front of them.

"Not so far."

Adam went on to describe the missing items, combining the information Ada gave him with that of Madeline Fox.

"I've seen Belknap paintings valued for as little as ten thousand dollars on the Antique Road Show," Catherine said.

"Perhaps the paintings and Mr. Trevelyan's information are a guide to something else, something more valuable, and he knew or suspected what it was?"

"Could be." Adam went on, "I promised you dinner. Would you and Catherine join me at Evan's tomorrow night?"

"I'd love to," Anne said.

"Oh, I can't," said Catherine. "I'm involved with something at the women's shelter."

"We'll do it another time. Would seven suit you, Anne?"

As it did, they agreed to meet at the restaurant, a pleasant walk from Catherine's.

An aristocratic Porsche, alien among the GM products parked in front of the courthouse, drew a crowd of three small boys, and one elderly man leaning on a cane. Adam noted the Quebec plates as he strode past it and up the stairs to the courthouse proper. The double oak doors to the Police Station's part of the building opened to give him a whiff of exotic perfume. Porsche and two hundred dollars-an-ounce perfume, he thought. What have we here?

Alisse Bertrand, tall and slender with the elegant flair many Frenchwomen seem to be born with, waited in his office. Dark eyes, vivid makeup, and lovely gold jewelry gave a stunning first impression. The second impression was of an angry or worried woman. Adam could see tension in the taut lines around her eyes and mouth, and the abrupt movement as she extended her hand.

"Detective Davidson, I'm Alisse Bertrand. John Andrews was my husband."

Even her voice, with a subtle accent, was elegant.

"My condolences, Ms. Bertrand. Would you mind answering a few questions?"

"Not at all, if I might ask some as well?"

"Of course. Do you know what brought him to Culver's Mills?"

"I...I think he was having an affair with a woman here."

"An affair. Why do you think so?"

An affair had not been on his list of possible motives for the murder, although in retrospect he supposed it should have been.

Her fingers tapped on the arm of her chair as she listed the reasons for suspecting her husband.

"Oh, the usual: phone calls with hanging up when I answered; unexplained or poorly excused weekends away. I brought the phone records from his office. Lots of calls to Vermont. Nothing in his e-mail that I could get into."

"You've been through this before?"

"Several times. I was leaving this time. I am, was fed up."

Her voice had some snap, but her eyes remained tired and downcast.

"Were you involved with his business?"

"Very little. I'm an artist, and he carried my paintings in his gallery, but I didn't have anything to do with the business side. Oh, I met the other artists at openings and some of the more important clients at our home, but that was all. Now, I suppose I must learn or close the gallery. The accountants, new ones, are going over the books."

"New ones? You didn't trust the ones who worked for him? Could you give me their names?"

"Yes." Her voice and face hardened. "I thought they were likely cheating John or cheating with him. The firm is called Charbonneau et Fils, but I never saw anyone of that name. I found a card," she said as she handed it to him.

"Thank you."

"You thought, think he was a criminal?"

"He's well known to the police in Montreal, but they couldn't prove anything."

"But he's never been arrested. There have been no police at the gallery."

She laced her shaking fingers together and held her hands in her lap.

"I know. The Montreal police reported they believe he's a fence and does some art thefts himself. Perhaps the weekends away weren't other women?"

Adam watched shock, and doubt play over her face.

She shook her head and said, "I think a woman as well."

"Did you bring the phone records with you?"

He hadn't noticed a briefcase, and her slim purse wouldn't hold much.

"I gave them to one of your officers. Do you have any more questions? I would like to go."

Sudden fatigue made her voice drag.

"Of course. Are you returning to Quebec?"

"Perhaps tomorrow. I need to make arrangements."

Her movements were fluid, like a model, he thought, as she stood, threw an incredibly thin shawl over her shoulders, and extended a hand.

"Good-bye, Lieutenant."

"Good-bye."

The phone records showed all the calls were made to phones in public areas in Burlington: office buildings, airports, bus stations. No chance of anyone remembering one individual. No two calls were ever made to the same phone.

"They must have prearranged calling times, maybe by e-mail," said Brad.

"Did we recover his computer?"

"Yes, she brought it with her. His e-mail's protected so I'll have to try to figure out a password."

"His widow couldn't get in. Won't be easy."

"I'll keep trying."

Adam left to check on Trevelyan at the hospital.

Chapter Twelve

With fishing over, Jamie Corrigan's thoughts turned to television and video games. Unfortunately for him, his parents insisted on school too, so he spent the day cooped up and restless with twenty other kids. He had endless patience for those activities he liked and none at all for sitting and writing. He did like to draw, though. The art assignment had been to draw a landscape. His effort included a lake and a fishing boat, with a half-submerged car in the distance. The teacher showed his picture, marked B, to the class. He didn't get too many B's. Something to show his parents.

He was going out to his grandparents' farm after school today. His route took him past the home of the class bullies, Kyle and Mike Bassett. His dad said they were meaner than junkyard dogs and they lived in a junkyard, too.

Jamie planned to leave school fast because the Bassett boys always stopped at the corner store. He could bike faster and be past their place before they got home. But the Bassetts were lying in wait as he left the school ground.

"Give us that drawing, you little jerk."

Kyle was bigger than Mike, sandy-haired and heavy- set. Mike was shorter and thinner, more like his mother and more of a follower. Dumber, too, thought Jamie.

"No."

Jamie didn't wait to hear an answer. He ran faster than the other boys and biked faster, and he had a better bike. He hadn't locked it to the bike stand but hidden it in a park across the road. There he fled, leaving the surprised Bassetts behind. They howled when he emerged at top speed.

Jamie's route out of town took him past old man Bassett's. Unless they called their dad to stop him, he would out-race them and make his grandpa's.

As he rounded the curve and came down the hill past the junk-yard, a man's burly figure came out of the house, holding a phone and watching the road. He's the guy who pushed the car, Jamie thought. He's coming after me. Now he was scared. Bassett couldn't run, but he might follow him in the truck.

Past the house, the road made a lazy S curve, and he would be out of Bassett's sight. A path through the bush was wide enough for a bike. The engine revved behind him, but he got off his bike and carried it into the underbrush, trying not to leave a trail. When Bassett roared by, Jamie flew off down the narrow track. He knew every inch. There was a hill to climb before the path spiraled down to the back of his grandpa's barn. The Bassett kids rode this trail, too. If their dad phoned them that he lost him, they might follow him up.

The trail had never been steeper, and Jamie had never ridden faster than now. When he reached halfway, he looked back at the road. Two figures, one in a red jacket, the other in a blue one, were turning onto the path. It was them, he thought. He could beat them; he knew he could.

The top of the climb wasn't as easy as the bottom. More rocks and tree roots grabbed his tires and threw him into skids. It was narrower too, easier for Jamie, harder for the bulkier Kyle Bassett.

They were shouting at each other, or maybe at him. When he

reached the crest, Jamie didn't stop but pedaled downhill faster than ever in his life. The track snaked back and around boulders and clumps of trees. Parts were muddy from the recent rain, and Jamie skidded into a half-fall as he rounded the final curve before Grandpa's field.

Jamie burst from the last copse of trees, startling his Grandpa's placid Holsteins, whose soft dark eyes stared at him as he barreled across the pasture. Now only the farmhouse field to go. He made it. He threw his bike to the ground and hurled himself through the green door into his grandmother's kitchen.

"Jamie, what on earth?"

The two other boys appeared from behind the trees, jumped off their bikes and stared at the house.

"Were those boys chasing you, Jamie?"

"Yes. I have to talk to Grandpa, Nan. I saw something I need to tell the police."

"I'll talk to him."

That was the nice thing about Nan; she never thought you were a silly kid.

Jamie ran to the front window to watch his Nan walk out to the gate. Grandpa was talking to some guy in a truck. Oh, no, he thought. That's old man Bassett. Now, Nan looked mad, throwing her arms out and pointing behind the house. She's telling him his boys chased me. Now Grandpa was yelling and pointing the way out the gate.

The truck wheels spun, sending up dirt. For a moment, Jamie couldn't see his grandparents, and then they walked like ghosts out of the dust.

The screen door bounced off the wall as his grandfather pushed into the kitchen.

"Jamie, what's going on? Bassett claims you took some picture from his sons."

"No, I didn't. I drew it myself in art class. Mrs. Marion gave me a B. They want it because I saw their dad shove an old car into the lake yesterday and I drew it."

Jamie's words tumbled over each other in his hurry to tell his story.

"Let me see it."

Jamie's grandfather was short, stocky and muscular and got red in the face when he was angry.

"Where is this, Jamie?"

"Grass Lake, at the bridge, where the deep hole is."

"He pushed a car in?"

"Yes."

Jamie flushed too, right to the roots of his red hair.

"I think we should call Lieutenant Davidson."

"How do you know Lieutenant Davidson?"

"He talked at our school."

"Let's call your dad."

Chapter Thirteen

The news at the hospital wasn't good. Adam spoke to Anita Morris, the nurse in charge in the ICU. She described Trevelyan as "hanging on". They had reversed the effects of the heroin, but he still had a severe chest injury on top of his underlying lung disease. It might be weeks before he weaned off the respirator.

"Can he talk?"

"Of course not, Adam. He's intubated and sedated."

"Let me know when he can at least manage yes and no."

"Alright."

She hung up, and Adam looked at the phone in surprise. He had known Anita most of their lives, and she wasn't usually that short with him. She must be anxious.

"Boss?"

"Yeah?"

"What about this guy Bassett who had access to the kid's backpack? Do you like him for the job?"

"Not on his own. Someone who knows art set it up. But he may have done the library theft. See if you can place him that night."

"Want me to go visit him?"

"Not yet."

The bells in the church opposite the courthouse were ringing one o'clock when Adam walked out of the courthouse and across the square to the travel agent's office. The agent, a woman called Janice Maynard, was new to town. Erin sat across from the woman, her short dark hair a contrast to Janice's flaming orange. Adam wondered what brought the agent o Culver's Mills. She'd fit in better in Oahu or Soho, with her orange hair and purple shirt.

Big voice too, he thought, as she boomed at him across the room.

"Adam, you made it. Come in. We have to decide if you want a big resort or a small hotel."

"Hi.

Adam shook hands with Janice.

"Whatever Erin wants."

"Adam, you have to be happy too," Erin said.

"That's what I said, whatever you want."

An hour later and after a quick lunch at Lil's, Adam walked back across the park to the courthouse. They decided on a bed and breakfast near a beach called Horseshoe Bay. One of the ten best beaches in the world, Janice assured them. He didn't care, as long as he had an uninterrupted week with Erin.

At his grandfather's farm, Jamie tried to convince his grandfather they couldn't wait for his dad.

"Grandpa, I saw him. I know I did. They know it too. I didn't tell the class who pushed in the car 'cause I didn't remember till I saw him, so they were chasing me cause they knew I saw him."

Jamie paused for breath. His grandpa was stubborn, and if he decided Jamie was wrong, that was it. But Grandpa wasn't saying anything, just sitting and looking at the picture.

They sat around the chrome and blue Arborite table waiting for

Jamie's dad to come. Every few minutes, Jamie ran to the front window, not, as his grandparents thought, to look for his father, but to look for Bassett. Jamie was afraid he would come back. In his video-fuelled imagination, he saw Kyle (age eleven) with an AK-47 aimed at his grandfather.

"Jamie, your dad said he would come out after work."

"Try to sit still and eat your cookies," Nan said.

"What if he comes back?"

"You're watching for Bassett?" Grandpa asked.

"Yes."

Grandpa picked up the phone and called Jamie's dad again.

"Pete, can you come out here? The situation may be more serious than I thought. Jamie's afraid Bassett is coming to hurt him, and we can't calm him down. No, I'd like you to here before we do that. Okay."

Oh, no, Jamie thought, he won't call the police until Dad comes.

It was almost five o'clock before Pete arrived. A square-built man with the same red hair as Jamie, Pete laid bricks and concrete blocks for a living and had the massive upper body that went with his trade. The happy yapping of two hounds and a retriever greeted his arrival.

"Jamie, what have you been up to this time?"

His dad was mad, Jamie thought, not recognizing that his father's anxiety made him seem angry.

"I drew what I saw, Dad. Then those Bassett kids tried to take the picture from me. Old man Bassett and some other guy shoved the car in the lake. I saw it, and now they're after me."

"Take it easy. We'll call the police, and you can tell them about it. "

Pete's thick fingers punched the numbers into the phone.

"Boss, you need to hear this," Brad said walking into Adam's office, handing over the phone as he spoke.

"Lieutenant Davidson, this is Pete Corrigan. My boy, Jamie, saw something you should hear about if you're looking for a missing car."

"Yes, we are. Do you want me to come out or are you coming in?"

"We'll come in. I have to bring Jamie home."

Ten minutes later a scared and excited Jamie was sitting in Adam's office telling his story.

"Are you sure it was Bassett?"

"Yes. He had on the same clothes."

"Did you know the other man?"

"No."

"Would you recognize him if you saw him again?"

"I don't know."

"That's okay, Jamie. What color was the car?"

"One of those old peoples' colors. Like Aunt Julie's?"

Jamie turned to his father for help.

"Beige, Lieutenant."

"Do you know cars? What make was it?"

"I don't know. It wasn't GM or Ford."

Adam looked at Pete Corrigan and then called the desk clerk to take Jamie for a Coke.

" We'll go out to the lake and search for the car. In the mean-time, could you take Jamie away on a little trip?"

Pete's color faded.

"You think that bastard will try to hurt Jamie?"

"People are dying."

"I'll take him and his mother to his grandparents in Montpelier. How long?"

"Plan on a week."

Adam's thought's turned to Bassett—access to the password for the computer system, an ugly temper, and pushing a car into the lake. Not enough to take to the judge, until they found the car. He swung his boots to the floor and collected Brad from the squad room. Twenty minutes later they were standing at the causeway.

"You fish, Brad?"

"Sure."

"Here?"

"All the time when I was a kid."

"Where's the deep hole?"

"Off the flat. If you're good, you can cast into it from right there."

Brad pointed towards the shore.

"Let's walk in from the road, but keep to the side for now."

Down at the flat, they read the traces of Jamie's story in the road—tire marks and men's footprints with tiny hillocks of dirt behind them from the effort of the push. Two sets of prints led away from the scene, one set deep with a long stride, the other shallower and shorter.

"We need a crew," Adam said. "I want casts of the prints and a diver right away to make sure no one is in the car."

"You think someone else got killed? You want me to go in now?"

"Possible. No, not you. It's too cold without a wet-suit."

More night work, Adam thought. The budget's going to be shot. But he couldn't count on weather holding off, and he needed those casts and the car out of the water. Brad walked back from the vehicle to join him. They stared at the dark water as they waited for the crew to arrive.

With tall pines as silent onlookers in the darkness, a tow truck raised the car from the water. Like a movie scene, Adam thought, complete with clanking chains, shouts of "take it easy" and the sucking, gurgling, bubbling sound as the car came out of the water. The diver couldn't come until morning, so they had gone ahead without knowing if the car was also a murder scene.

When they got the car on land, Brad popped the trunk. No body. The interior revealed the disguise—hospital greens, mask and badge.

"Bag it all. Maybe we can recover DNA from something. Take the car to the impound lot and call the lab boys from Burlington for the morning. Maybe we can tie the car to Bassett."

"Will do."

It had been a long day. Time to go home and feed Sam.

Chapter Fourteen

Anne nestled further under one of Catherine's endless supply of Afghan comforters. Catherine was turning over one of her raised vegetable garden beds, but Anne was forbidden to help.

The phone on the table beside her rang. A querulous voice asked for Catherine.

"Catherine, phone for you."

Catherine wiped the worst of the soil off her hands and walked up the three steps to the porch.

"You don't seem too fond of whomever that was," Anne said when she finished the call.

"Dan Abbott, the librarian in Brownsville. The word for him is mean-spirited."

Catherine sat on the bench that formed one side of the deck.

"Ouch. That's why you aren't available? How do you know him?"

"All I ever did was have lunch with him one day after a library board meeting. He spent the entire time telling me how clever he was and how he manipulated his library board. He keeps calling, and I keep putting him off."

"Are you looking for a relationship?"

"Maybe, but not with him. I might go back to school when the boys do since you are helping me with their expenses. I don't think I'll ever be able to thank you enough."

"Going back to school is a good idea. What would you take?"

"Law is what interests me. I could do the LSAT, and apply for the part-time degree Adam's doing."

"Good for you. You organized the antique show, I understand?"

"Yes. Are you going to be able to come over?"

"Sure. I'm having dinner with Adam, so I'll not stay long. I tire quickly."

"I'm sure. Speaking of men, are you going to see Thomas again while you are here?"

"I saw Thomas again, and that did not go well."

"What happened?"

Catherine picked the last of the flowers from the petunias in the planters while Anne described the quarrel to her.

"...and I feel so badly about it. The nurse told me he sat there for hours, watching me breathe."

"Nonetheless, it isn't his business."

Catherine dumped her handful of crushed petals destined for the compost into a basket.

"I'm not sure where we are in this relationship, or even if there is one after that episode."

"Take it as it comes."

"I guess. I want to visit James Trevelyan this morning. I wonder if they would let me in the ICU. Meantime, I think I'm going to nap here in the sun."

"I'm sure they would. Enjoy yourself. I'm going to finish the vegetable bed and top up the compost heap."

Catherine walked down to the garden. Anne slept.

Later that afternoon, when Anne arrived at the intensive care, she found the staff quite willing to let her come in, even though she wasn't a relative. They told her no one except police had been in, and she was on the list of permitted visitors.

She sat beside the bed in the familiar surroundings. A monitor flashed green messages from its elevated perch. The ventilator is very quiet, she thought, watching the rhythmic movement of the old man's chest. He's so helpless. He would hate that if he knew. Pale too, but at least opening his eyes now from time to time. Another day and they would try to wean him off the ventilator. Anne talked to him, telling him about her research and what she discovered about his family. Sometimes it helped to hear a familiar voice, familiar names.

Anne noticed a slight stirring when she spoke, but no real arousal. That was to be expected, though, when he was sedated because of the ventilator. Telling the staff that she would be back the next day, she left after twenty minutes. She always found sitting at a bedside, unable to work with the patient, exhausting. Frustration, she supposed, or a feeling of impotence.

The walk to the diner took Anne along tree-shaded streets with century homes set back in expansive lawns. Her mood didn't improve in spite of the signs of spring. She came to Vermont for a holiday and here she was, investigating crime again. The fear was starting to get old.

On her last visit she'd been hurtled down a cliff by a car pushing her off the road, shot at, near-drowned and all to find out who killed a blackmailing woman. The murderer turned out to be more sympathetic than the victim. No wonder the jury and the judge were lenient. Now the victim was a thief and who knows what else.

Why should she waste her time here? She wanted to visit with her friends, sketch a little, see where the relationship with Thomas was going—apparently not far—and that was because she came here. If she had seen him in Toronto, there would have been no nasty scene. What was the matter with her? The man cared, and she treated him as though he wanted to shut her in a house without sunshine. Perhaps, she thought again she'd go home.

After lunch at the diner, she went on to the antique show at the Legion Hall. Anne was familiar with the Legion at home, attending events as diverse as weddings and wakes, as well as other antique shows. The hall was much the same—different flags, different uniforms on the mannequins, same worn-down decor under low ceilings.

A line-up at the door forecast a successful show. Anne paid her two dollars and searched for Catherine. She found her deep in conversation with an elderly man at a table covered with old kitchen utensils and pots. She waved and started around the booths.

Tables and booths filled every available piece of floor space. Jammed was the word. Dealers liked it that way, so she had been told. Perhaps it encouraged people to slow down, look at things more carefully. In the past, she found a few treasures on the floor, under the tables, hidden in baskets or behind larger objects. Anne had developed a personal strategy—once around the room to check out what was available and a second time, stopping at the booths that interested her.

Antique costume jewelry sparkled from the cases in booth one. Catherine joined Anne as she held a leaf-shaped brooch, glittering with green and blue brilliants.

"I didn't know you liked this sort of thing, Anne."

"My mother did. We spent a summer visiting antique stores in small towns in the Valley. I've looked at many different pieces, some of it well made. Certain signatures make it more valuable, I understand, but I don't know much about it."

She returned the piece to the dealer with a smile.

"Shall we walk around?" Catherine said.

"Sure."

"Oh, no."

Catherine swung back, almost colliding with Anne.

"What's the matter?"

"Dan Abbott came in. You know, the one on the phone this morning. Stay with me, Anne. Don't be polite and leave."

"I'll cling like a limpet."

He does look a little mean, she thought. Smiles with his mouth, not his eyes. She listened to Catherine's frosty greeting, shook Abbott's offered hand, and lingered even though he expected her to leave.

"I'm showing Anne around at the moment. Perhaps later."

Abbott finally moved off.

"You'd think I encouraged him, and I swear I haven't."

"Forget it. You can be too busy all day."

"That's true enough."

At that, one of the volunteers bustled up with a problem only Catherine could deal with and led her away. Anne continued around the hall. One or two booths carried old linen. She preferred to buy and use antique linen because of the interesting patterns and generous sizes. Those yellowed with age bleached to pristine whiteness.

Next to the linen booths, a wizened little woman sold orientalia. A tiny red clay teapot caught Anne's eye. This sort of pottery was called Yi Xing. Teapots formed from the zisha clay found in Yi Xing, China, had been made for hundreds of years, since the Sung Dynasty when the purple clay used for their manufacture was first discovered. Anne loved them but had only one. Twenty dollars. That was about what she had paid before and much less than the going rate. The oldest ones had a wonderful patina and an unglazed interior. The color and the modeling seemed authentic, right down to the ladybug on a leaf.

As Anne leaned over the table, she felt a sudden fear and a flash of memory of James's crumpled body on the grass. What brought that on? She was alone in the booth. The dealer chatted with her next-door neighbor. Two women were discussing the plates in the booth behind her. Several people were moving past her down the aisle. A heavy scent, White Diamonds, or something like that, drifted over. No murderers in sight. Giving herself a mental shake, Anne returned to the teapot and negotiated a better deal.

Antique jewelry was up next. Most of what the dealer had dated from the Victorian age, and not very good Victorian at that: seed pearls and poor turquoise, buckle rings and mourning brooches.

One piece of geometric design in burnished platinum and diamonds stood out from the other, more modest offerings. Seventy-five dollars. A low price.

"Where did this come from?" she asked the dealer, a plump, sweater-clad man of about fifty.

"Consignment."

"Not your usual period?"

"No. My aunt asked me to sell it for her. It's a lovely piece."

It was always an aunt or a granny or a dying friend, Anne thought. She hoped it wasn't stolen.

"Can you do better?" she asked, knowing the answer would be no.

"No, it's not mine."

"All right."

It was too lovely to leave behind, and it was undervalued. Anne excused her purchase to herself as she paid the seventy-five. Catherine returned as she walked past the last booth (toys and dolls).

"Are you going around again?" Catherine asked.

"No, I spent more than I intended."

She showed Catherine her brooch and teapot.

"The strangest thing happened."

Anne went on to tell Catherine about the flashback.

"Was anyone around you?"

"Two women talking in the booth behind me, and a bunch of people in the aisle. There was a heavy scent in the air.

"Who were the women?"

"I don't know. I'll point them out if I see them again."

"Let's sit down."

The tables had filled with shoppers by the time they reached the lunch room, staffed by volunteers from the Women's Shelter. She'd never notice those women in this crush, Anne thought. She couldn't go around sniffing everyone. She sipped her drink and watched the crowd. Serious collectors inspected marks and provenance. Young children spent small change on animal figurines or hair ornaments. A politician strolled by complete with wife, their baby in a stroller decorated with a campaign sign, and the family retriever sporting the party's colors in a neckerchief. As much fun as a fair.

"Are you staying?"

Catherine broke into her thoughts.

"No, I'm tired. I need a nap before going out to dinner tonight with Adam. Life here is a social whirl."

"We stay open until eight tonight."

"Your hours are a little different than usual?"

"Yes, they are. We are so out-of-the-way that I like to give the dealers the first morning to get here. We stay open late the first night, close at five the second and at noon the final day to let them leave early. No thanks," she said as she shook her head at the server.

"Are there any other events in town on now?"

"No. What did you have in mind?"

"If you're attracting people from other states, across the border, or from Burlington, you might get them to linger in town if you also had something at the theatre and a show at the gallery. A fall festival, perhaps, with house tours, autumn decorations in the stores, special sales. The sort of thing they do in Elora. You've been to Elora?"

Elora was a picturesque village in Mennonite country in rural Ontario.

"Years ago."

"How are plans for the mill coming along? Elora's is a private inn and restaurant."

"Not well. It's derelict, and the town hasn't committed to help with the fund-raising."

"I saw scaffolding?"

"Yes, it needed some emergency repairs."

"Who owns it?"

"The Culvers. They are doing the temporary repairs. They have offered to sell it to the town for one dollar if the money can be raised to renovate it or restore it."

"And so?"

"Quite a few people don't want to use tax money for the "arty" stuff," Catherine said with a wry smile.

"Ah. I've heard that one before. Lots of money for sports fields and Christmas decoration, but nothing for the arts."

"That's about it."

"I'd like to see the mill before I go home."

"Sure. I can arrange that for you."

"Thanks.

As Anne walked out through a side door, she glimpsed Abbott again, this time talking to a mousy-haired woman whom Anne recognized as the librarian, Nancy Webb. She hoped he wouldn't continue to bother Catherine, she thought. She started her car and headed back to the bed and breakfast and a nap.

Thomas's beloved car—a little two-seater silver Honda Prelude—sat in front of the house. When she drove into the driveway, he got up from one of the wicker chairs on the veranda and walked down the stairs to meet her. She's exhausted, he thought.

"Hi," he said, holding out his arms.

Anne went to him, was enfolded in a fierce hug, and smiled up into his face as he bent down to kiss her.

"Hi. Come inside for a drink."

"I only have a few minutes, Anne. I have to go to New York on business."

"Come up and sit for a minute then."

When they reached the chairs and sat, Anne said, "I'm sorry I was so nasty in the hospital."

"Nasty? You weren't nasty but you were right; I had no business tackling Davidson. I was so worried about you."

He reached over and took Anne's hand. "I'd like us to see more of each other. I hope that is still okay with you?"

"Very okay."

Thomas glanced at his watch and stood up.

"I have to go. I'll call you from New York."

"I'll be out for a while this evening."

Remembering not to ask where, Thomas kissed her, strode down to his car, folded himself into the front seat and drove away.

Chapter Fifteen

Adam found a file marked Bassett on his desk in the morning. Brad had been busy. The car in the lake was wiped clean of prints, but he found one thumbprint on the underside of the trunk lid. Not enough to be definitive but a good match for Bassett. With Jamie's evidence, enough to bring Bassett in.

Responding solo was not Adam's style, not anymore. Years ago a bullet in his leg put him out for six months. With backup was how he played it now.

"No lights, no sirens. Pull up out on the road first. If Bassett sees us, he may run. I don't want the wife and kids in the way."

Bassett's big semi cab was missing.

"Okay, turn into the lane, Pete. Brad," he called to the car behind, "follow us in but stay back with the vehicle."

"In or out?"

"Out."

No dog. Strange, Adam thought. Last time, the dog, a German Shepherd cross chained out by the Quonset hut, never shut up.

"Think he's taken off, boss?"

"Looks like it, but be careful. I'll do the door. You watch the back."

Adam waited until Pete reached the corner of the house, and then he pounded on the front door, standing well to the side.

"Mrs. Bassett. Adam Davidson, Culver Police. I'd like to talk to you."

Silence again. Dog's not inside, he thought. No boys either. They weren't at school. He'd checked before coming out.

"Mrs. Bassett, are you all right?"

The inside door stood open. A small foyer, crowded with sports equipment, opened into a hall that led straight through to the back door. A figure appeared against the light. Mrs. Bassett, but moving slowly. She was injured, he thought. What was her first name? Nora.

"I'm coming to help you, Nora. Is he here?"

"No," the faint voice came. "No."

Her bruised left eye was swollen shut. Blood trailed down her face from a split in the skin overlying her cheekbone. More blood oozed from her upper lip over a deformed lower jaw. She collapsed into him as he came up to her.

"Brad, call an ambulance," he said into his shoulder radio.

When she spoke, Adam could see missing and broken teeth.

"My boys," she whispered. "He took my boys."

"Where did he go, Nora? We'll go after him."

"I don't know," her voice trailed off as she drifted into unconsciousness.

"Nora, Nora, wake up. Talk to me."

Her eyes flickered. "So tired. Maybe the cabin, beyond Tyrone, on Bass Lake. He has a gun."

She left him again.

"Brad, APB on the semi. A man and two boys. Maybe towards Tyrone. Armed and very dangerous."

A faint pulse still flickered at her wrist, but her breathing was irregular as the paramedics reached her. Adam had watched this procedure many times but rarely felt the cold anger that flooded him now. Anger towards Bassett, yes, but not a little toward the pale figure on the stretcher. They were bagging her now. Why hadn't she come with him when he was out here before? It had been a matter of time with a guy like Bassett.

"She's bad," said the paramedic as they left. "Is there any family other than the guy who did this?"

"A daughter. She's sixteen. Two young boys."

"Tough."

He had attacked her in her kitchen. The overturned chairs, broken dishes, the table pushed back against the sink, a hank of bloody hair lying on the floor—Nora fought back this time. The phone dangled off the wall. He punched redial and got the 911 operator. Someone tried, maybe one of the sons.

"Davidson, Culver police. Did you take a call from this number?"

"Yes, but the father said it was a kid, pranking."

"Now it's a woman, dying. I'll be in touch."

He dialed Ada Warren.

"Ada, Adam Davidson. Do you have Chrissy home today?"

"No, she's at school. What's happened?"

"Her mom's badly hurt. Can you take Chrissy to the hospital? I'm going after the dad. He won't be there."

"Yes, I will. Did he do it?"

"Yes."

Chapter Sixteen

The small village of Tyrone lay fifty miles east and north towards Canada. A lake bordered the road that ran through the village. Two trailer parks, one more upscale and permanent than the other, a museum set back in lovely gardens, a restaurant and a gas station along with a church and a street of well-kept homes comprised the whole place. Adam stopped at the four corners and talked to the man at the pumps.

"Yeah, Bassett, that s.o.b. He came through here about three hours ago, driving the cab from his big rig. He took out the corner when he left," he said, pointing to a battered retaining wall.

"Which way?"

"Turned left. His place is on the lake. Go up three miles and turn right. After that, I don't know exactly."

"Thanks."

On the way, Adam called the sheriff of the county, Prescott Jones, a classmate of Adam at the Academy ten years before. He would send some men.

After they left the main highway, they had to slow to a crawl. Calling it a road was a stretch, Adam thought. Broken and fallen branches marked the passage of the semi. A white, shattered trunk marked the turn into what Adam assumed was the lane into the cabin.

"We taking the cruiser in?" Pete asked.

"Not too far."

The boys were the problem. Would Bassett use his sons as hostages or kill them and himself, or give up? He was a belligerent drunk and wife-beater.

"What about this guy, Pete? Will he give up?"

"Depends. We've had to tie him down to throw him in the drunk tank. He goes ballistic. If he's sober, I don't know."

"The daughter said he gave everything to "his boys". Maybe he'll give up to save them."

"I'd bet he'd use them to try and save himself. He's a real son of a bitch."

Inside the cabin, the level in the bottle was getting lower. The two boys, familiar with their dad when he was drinking, sat as far away as possible and kept as quiet as possible. The dog huddled close to them. He knew too.

Mike whispered to Kyle, "Mom was hurt bad."

"Shush, he'll hear you."

"I'm scared. I want to go home."

"Don't cry. He might start on us. There's no one left but us."

"What if Mom is dead?"

Mike muffled his sobs with his jacket sleeve.

"Shut up, you brats. I'm trying to think," he shouted at the boys, and muttered on to himself, "That fucking bitch. How did he get into this? Easy money, she said. No problem. In and out. Now it's murder."

He reached to fill his glass up again. Empty. The bottle bounced off the door and onto the floor.

The boys huddled closer. Now he was out of liquor. If he went to buy more, they could run away, thought Kyle. He could find his way to town; he knew he could.

Bassett shook his bovine head. His small eyes reddened. At that moment Adam called him through his bullhorn.

"Bassett. Davidson from Culver's Mills police. I know you're in there. Let the boys out. No one else has to get hurt today."

"Fuck off, cop."

Bassett's shotgun smashed the window and pointed at the sound. Adam had strung a microphone wire from the horn to where he and Pete sheltered behind an outcropping of rock.

"Your wife's hurt bad. I need to take the boys to her."

A blast from the shotgun echoed through the trees as it shattered the windshield of the cruiser.

"Let the boys out, Bassett."

"No, they're mine. They're staying with me."

Another blast.

"He's lost it, Adam," said Pete.

"This is how he gets."

"How long does he take to sober up?"

"A day. If we wait him out, he loses the rage and starts crying, real remorseful."

"How long does this stage last?"

"Couple, three hours."

"Too long. We need to get the boys out. Check if there's a back way in. Circle wide."

Adam used his cell to call the sheriff and tell him it was now a hostage situation.

Pete doubled back past the cruiser and went to the right through the trees. Long minutes passed before he came up behind Adam and slumped down beside him, panting, resting the shotgun he had taken from the cruiser across his legs.

"It fronts on the lake. Some cover for him, if he runs for it. There's a dock with a powerboat tied up.

"Any way out of this lake by boat?"

"No."

"He may ask for a plane. Call for a float plane on standby."

"Bassett, let the boys come out."

"No."

Again the shotgun blasted, hitting a tree and leaving bark hanging in shreds.

Inside the cabin, Bassett's blurred eyes moved slowly around the room. Going to have to block off the windows, he thought. Got to make a stand. What the hell, take a few with him. Where was his rifle? He was sure he brought the rifle. Kids. Christ, why'd he bring the kids?

"Go hide in the bunk room. Stay away from the window. Take the damn dog with you."

The boys scrambled to their feet, dragging the dog with them.

"Close the damn door."

Mike sobbed in the corner of the room

"He's going to keep shooting at the cops, Kyle. I want to get out of here."

"Shut up. I have to think."

Kyle could think better. Mike sat on the bunk while Kyle prowled the little room. Double bunks with stained and worn mattresses stood against two sides. They could stack the mattresses up to stop the bullets. Packing cases were piled up against the back wall. Inside, he found mostly clothes. Hunting jackets and caps.

Boots. His dad and his buddies used the cabin when they went duck hunting.

Kyle continued his survey. Two small screws held the window in. They could take it out and get away.

Maybe they shouldn't leave Dad, but the cops were going to shoot. Kyle watched hours of television, and he knew the SWAT team would arrive soon, and they would have no chance. When his dad was like this, you couldn't talk to him. He wouldn't give up. Not till he was sober, and they would all be dead. He wanted his mother. He knew she was hurt bad.

"Stop crying and help me move these boxes so we can climb on them."

"What are we going to do?"

"Leave."

The boys shifted the boxes and stacked them under the window. Kyle climbed up and used his little pocketknife to twist out the screws that held the window in place. It stuck a little, but he was able to take it out of the frame without making too much noise. The next room was quiet. Had his dad passed out? He was afraid to look.

"Mike, I'll boost you. Wait for me right by the cabin."

"What if the cops shoot me?"

"It's Davidson, the one that came to the school. He won't shoot a kid. Don't you remember?

"Oh, yeah."

"Now, go."

When Mike cleared the window, Kyle pushed the dog through the window after him. He piled another box on to the stack. Was his Dad coming? Fear took him up and through the window. When he hit the ground, he dragged Mike from the shelter of the cabin's wall and ran left away from the window and the shooting. He could hear another burst from the shotgun as they reached the edge of the clearing. A few minutes later, the trees closed around them, and the sun disappeared. It wasn't dark yet, but there was no trail to follow.

Kyle kept moving in what he thought was a straight line. Now and then he could see the lake.

Adam and Pete didn't see the boys leave. Adam decided not to talk to Bassett until backup arrived. Always the chance he would pass out.

Behind them, three cruisers turned into the narrow lane.

"Scotty," Adam shook his hand as the tall, thin sheriff folded himself down beside the rock, a smile briefly relieving his cadaveric face. "Good to see you."

"Rather it was somewhere else, Adam. What's the situation?"

"Guy in the cabin called Bassett. Ran up here with his sons, ten and eleven. Left his wife bruised and bleeding. Paramedics didn't think she'd make it."

"Will he talk to you?"

"Only with a shotgun."

"Give me the horn."

"Here's the microphone. We strung a wire. He fires at the voice."

"Bassett. Prescott Jones, County Sheriff. The time to come out is now. A SWAT team is on the way. Send those boys out now."

"No."

No shot. A step forward, Adam thought. Or he's saving ammo.

"Let me see they're all right."

"I'll look after my boys," Bassett roared.

"Like you looked after your wife? Let them go, Bassett."

Dead air. Jones turned to Adam. "Do you think we should tell him how bad she is?"

"I don't know him well enough."

Bassett sat back at the table, cradling the gun. What had he meant, "Like you took care of your wife"? She couldn't be dead. He didn't hit her that hard. No harder than before. She deserved it anyway. Saying she was taking the boys away. They were his. He loved them, his sons. Tears filled his bloodshot eyes. He looked around, trying to find them. He remembered that he had sent them into the bunk-room. They were quiet—no crying. He lumbered across the room and listened. He couldn't hear them. The open window, the stacked boxes and an empty room confronted him when he opened the door.

"No," he bellowed in rage and fired into the stack of boxes that had helped the boys escape.

"He's firing at the back of the cabin. Do you have anyone back there, Adam," asked Jones.

"Pete, over there on the right where he can watch the dock. A powerboat's tied up."

The radio crackled.

"The back door's open but I can't see him yet. Do you want me to shoot him if he runs?" said Pete.

"Do you think you can take him down without killing him?"

"I'm not that good, Adam."

"No shooting if he has the kids."

Bassett had sobered up enough to try to make a plan. He had gassed up the boat last time he was up here. If he could make the landing at the far end of the lake, he might make it away. Later he would come back for the boys. Kyle would stay away from the cops for a while, but eventually, they would be back in Culver's. All it would take was a little time to get them back.

He needed stuff if he had to go into the woods. Working quickly, he put together a pack, slung his rifle over his shoulder, and held his shotgun in his hand. There was enough cover between him and the cops that they wouldn't be able to tell if the boys were with him until he had reached the boat.

Pete saw the figure running towards the boat, and shot. He missed and dove behind trees and rock as Bassett's rifle shots ricocheted around him. He must have cut the ropes, Pete thought, as the boat drifted away from the dock and the engine caught. The end of the dock covered Basset as he backed the boat out.

"Boss, he took off up the lake," Pete called.

"Okay," Jones said, "only one place to dock. We'll get him." He spoke to his men as he ran to his vehicle.

Adam entered the cabin from the front, calling to Pete as he went in the door. "You didn't see the kids, did you?"

"No. I thought they were still in there."

The smells of cordite and cheap whiskey mingled with that of years of men and smoke and stale food in the cabin. Adam walked into the bedroom. The stacked boxes and window neatly placed against the wall told him what the boys had done.

"Are they dead?" Pete said.

"No, the place is empty. We're going to have to search the woods. It'll be night soon. Call search and rescue and let's see if you and I can follow them."

Two little boys didn't leave much of a trail. Adam wondered if one of them was smart enough to keep the lake in sight as they walked. He saw fresh signs of the dog. Good he was with them.

"Kyle, Mike. It's Lieutenant Davidson. You know me. Come out and talk to me."

Nothing, except the startled flight of birds higher in the trees. The deeper into the woods they went, the darker it became.

"We're walking blind. We should go back and wait for the dogs," Pete said.

"Okay."

Chapter Seventeen

"Erin, it's Adam. I need a favor."

"What's the matter?"

"I'm up at Tyrone. We're searching for the two Bassett boys, so I can't meet Anne for dinner. Would you mind going with her?"

"Of course not. What time? And were you meeting her at the restaurant or picking her up?"

"Seven, and I was going to meet her. Thanks, Erin.

Love you."

And he was gone.

"Love you too."

She was beginning to realize what a policeman's wife coped with. It was 6:45 p.m.

It was past 7:00 p.m. when Erin walked up the three steps and across the porch to Evan's front door.

A mirror above a flower-painted console table, reflecting the glow of a ruby-glass shaded lamp, spilled hues of red-gold across the faded oriental carpet in the foyer. Erin paused to enjoy the picture. On the table, Mary had replaced a butter-bowl filled with her collection of carpet balls, with a small grouping of Meito china—two bowls and a plate decorated with hand-painted fantasy birds and deep pink flowers. Not particularly valuable, Erin thought. Mary has thought better of displaying her treasures.

Mary and Andre opened three rooms for visitors. They offered breakfast and dinner, making it a very French-style boutique hotel, not a bed and breakfast.

Matilde appeared, tacking around the tables, her tight server's jacket emphasizing her more than substantial curves. Always reminded her of a figurehead on a ship, Erin thought.

"Good evening, Ms. Maxwell. Table for one?"

"Good evening, Matilde. No, I'm meeting Dr. McPhail. Is she here yet?"

"Yes, but I placed her at a table for two. Will you be joining her and Lieutenant Davidson?"

The arch tone of her voice irritated Erin.

"No, I'll be replacing Lieutenant Davidson."

Matilde drew back a little, realizing her error.

Erin followed her across the room to the small table near the fireplace she and Adam called theirs. The color scheme drawn from the foyer continued in here, with vibrant red tablecloths set off by brass-and-glass table lamps and royal blue napkins. Anne sat facing into the room. Adam wouldn't have liked that, Erin thought. He never sat with his back to others.

"Hi, Anne. I'm so sorry, but Adam can't make it."

"Oh, that's a shame. He's all right, is he?"

"Yes, but he can't get back in time."

"An opportunity for us to get to know each other better."

The conversation initially centered on their obsessions, antiques and genealogy, but then ranged into the international situation— which was frightening, as usual— and then the murder and missing artwork.

"Are you any closer to finding out if Mr. Trevelyan is the actual heir to this place and the painting?" Erin asked in a low tone as

Matilde hovered nearby. Service had been outstanding after her initial gaffe.

"Perhaps later," Anne said, indicating the server with a slight movement of an eyebrow.

"I think I'll go to the ladies' room."

A short hall off the foyer led into a tiny antechamber ornamented with a gilt-edged mirror and a papier-maché table. Both stalls were occupied, so Anne sat and touched up her makeup as she waited. A conversation was going on, too loud to ignore.

"How much were you offered for the place, Mary?"

"A lot more than it's worth. Three hundred thousand dollars."

"Three hundred. Why?"

"I have no idea, especially after the fire."

"You had a fire?"

"A small one, in a shed in the backyard. Matilde saw it and called the fire department. They said it had been deliberately set."

"No. How did they get past the dog in the yard?"

"I don't know."

Noises indicated the occupants of the stalls were soon to emerge. Anne slipped out and hurried back to her table. She sat before Mary entered the room and came over to speak to them.

"I hope you ladies had a good evening?"

"Everything was excellent, thank you," said Erin as she gave Mary her credit card.

"Let's split it."

"Oh, no. Adam will pay me back. Dinner's on him."

Anne watched to see who else emerged from the ladies' room, but no one reentered the dining room by the time they left.

Chapter Eighteen

Mike whimpered again when he heard the voice calling them.

"Why don't we wait for them? They'll take us to Mom."

"They'll put us into foster care. Remember last time?"

Mike remembered last time and was quiet.

"Why aren't there any sounds? Where are the birds?"

"They go to bed at night, dummy."

Kyle was scared now, too. With the light gone, he couldn't see the lake. Maybe they walked in circles.

Tall pines loomed overhead, blocking the sky and any hopeful glimpses of moon or stars. Bushes and roots grabbed at their legs; branches stung their faces and caught in their hair. Kyle was not an imaginative child, but he felt as though the forest was attacking him, holding him back so they would capture him. Mike fell and cried again.

They stumbled on, fell into a creek, and trudged along in the water for what seemed like miles before finding a place where they could climb out.

A light flashed through the trees ahead of them. Searchers? No one called.

"Mike, we have to be quiet and see what the light is."

"What if it's the police?"

"We'll be quiet until they go."

The light wasn't moving; Kyle was sure. He crept forward, dragging Mike with him. A tiny building loomed in front of them, but it was in darkness. The light came from beyond it.

The moonlight flooded a clearing, shining on a cabin and the lake beyond. The light in the cabin flickered as a figure passed back and forth beyond the window. Kyle couldn't hear anybody talking or yelling and only saw the shape of one person. That's a woman, he thought. Maybe she would help them.

Knowing he had to move closer, he whispered, "You stay here while I look in the windows."

"No, Kyle, no. Don't leave me. I'm coming too."

Mike panicked, grabbing at Kyle's arm and tugging on his jacket.

"Okay. Okay. Don't make any noise. No talking and no crying."

The boys crept around the edge of the clearing, oblivious to the dog chained beside the back door, and to the low warning growls deep in the throat of their dog. As they neared the cabin, the chained dog exploded into frantic barking. Kyle grabbed the collar of his dog as he flew past on the attack. Ahead of him, the screen door of the cabin flew open and the sudden light trapped the boys.

"I have a rifle aimed at you. Come in here."

"Don't shoot us, lady. Don't shoot us," Mike said.

"We're lost," Kyle said. "Can you help us?"

"Walk in here. Quiet, Tark," she said to the dog.

The boys crept forward, holding tight to their dog.

"What are you kids doing out here? Are you alone?"

"Yes," said Kyle. "We're lost, and we're freezing. We fell into a creek."

"Come in the house."

Adam waited for search-and-rescue to arrive. Based in Burlington, they were going to take quite a while to reach the scene. He also waited for word from Jones about Bassett. The taciturn sheriff said they'd get Bassett, but as Adam understood the geography, there was only one marina on the lake. Bassett hunted these woods all his life. He could beach the boat and disappear into the empty country between the lake and Canada.

Out in the middle of the lake, Bassett cut his engine and listened. No other sounds on the lake so no pursuit. Christ, why did he drink so much? He had to think. What would the cops do? The wharves on the lake were two miles further on. They would have cruisers waiting and put a boat in the water. He had to escape the lake and into the woods.

His buddy owned a cabin along here on the east shore. He'd dock and plan a route into the mountains and across the border. It was still open country at the border, even after 9/11. He drifted towards shore, restarted his engine, and chugged along the bank, watching for familiar landmarks.

Pale dawn light crept between the trees where Adam and Pete sat and waited. Nothing in the cabin belonged to the boys, so the dogs couldn't tell one scent from another. Adam rousted Brad out of bed and sent him around to Bassett's home to collect some of the children's clothing.

"Why did those kids run? Why not hide in the bushes, waiting for it to be all over?"

"Afraid of us."

"Why? I mean why in particular?"

"Foster home."

"What?"

"Two years ago it happened. The mom had an accident and was in hospital. Bassett was doing three months for assaulting some guy in a bar. The kids went to foster homes. The social workers separated the boys. The older one kept running away to the younger one. It lasted a month until the mom went home. I was with the children services worker who took them out of their home. It wasn't good."

"They're going to look for someplace to hide?"

"Yeah. The older one is smart enough. I don't think he'll panic."

A sudden blast from the radio told them Bassett escaped. They found his boat adrift, but there was no way of telling where he went to ground.

Chapter Nineteen

Local media crowded the entrance to the courthouse as a glowering Captain Naismith read a terse statement about the lost boys and their disappearing father. Atkins had sniffed out the attack on Trevelyan and his apparent death.

"Is this related to the murder at the hospital, Captain?"

"Not to our knowledge."

"What about to the thefts at the library?"

"Again, not that we know. The investigations are ongoing."

"What are you doing to find the boys?" asked a local television news reporter.

"Search-and-rescue, some of my officers, and some from the county are up there, Angie."

"What about getting help from the public?"

"If someone wants to help, call the sheriff's office in Kirk County. The search is in their jurisdiction. That's all. Thanks."

Oblivious to the reporters' shouted questions, he disappeared inside the courthouse.

Over at Lil's, excited conversation at every table had too many topics: murder at the hospital, the missing boys, a daring escape, the theft at the library. Behind the counter, Peg watched and listened. There were people in today who rarely showed until lunchtime, or not at all. Nancy Webb, now, Peg hadn't taken her for a sensationalist, but there she was, all ears. Fragments of the conversations drifted over the counter.

"Debbie, how's everyone at the hospital taking the murder?"

"What murder?"

"I hear those boys know something about the dead guy at LaPorte's."

"Murdered out at the Red Roof, they say, while he was in bed."

"The wife's in town."

As Peg walked out to the booths to serve her orders, she overheard speculation as well.

"You hear about the fire at Evan's?"

"They say it was arson."

"What's going on in this town?"

Lots of gossip and some fear, Peg thought. She hoped Adam made some progress soon. All the crime seemed to be wearing on Nancy Webb, judging by her pale face and shaking hands when she paid her bill. Maybe the board was threatening to fire her because of the robbery.

Lil's did brisk business all day, with people dropping in after visiting the antique show at the Legion. Quite a few made their way across to Erin's shop and even to Todd James, her neighbor whose window advertised "decorating hints".

Erin was finishing her morning chores—dusting, rearranging disturbed items, and setting up her cash— when the front door rattled. It wasn't yet ten o'clock, her opening time. The bubbled old glass in the heavy oak door distorted and blurred the figure beyond, but Erin easily recognized Dan Abbott's unwelcome face. What did he want at this hour? Reluctantly, she turned over her closed sign and opened the door, setting off a tinkling cascade of sound from the nest of bells above it.

"Good morning, Erin. I wondered if I could look round the shop before I went home?"

"Certainly, come in."

Dan Abbott had been an irregular visitor to the shop, always looking. Erin couldn't remember him buying anything, but he took up her time, gossiping. She had no idea why he was so interested in Culver's Mills. Maybe he wanted Nancy's job. Erin sat on the library board as a representative of its fund-raising foundation.

"What's new?" he said.

"What I'm sure you heard over at Lil's. How did you like the show at the Legion?"

She hoped to divert the steady questioning she knew was coming. The man should have been a reporter.

"Well, the best people, like yourself, aren't attending. I assume that's why you passed it up?"

Slimy, Erin thought.

"Certainly not. There are some fine dealers here. I don't do shows."

"Did you buy?"

"Yes, a few things."

"What did you find?"

"Some linens, and a lovely vase I think is Loetz."

Erin watched Abbott wander about the shop. He stopped at her locked case.

"Is this it?"

"Yes."

"It is lovely. You have exquisite taste."

"Thank you."

"Why are you burying yourself here. I'm sure you could do well in Montpelier or Burlington."

"I like the small-town life."

"I hear you have a romantic entanglement as well. With a policeman?"

The note of incredulity in his voice irritated her.

"I can't imagine why you are so interested, Dan."

"I suppose he's very busy with the robbery at the library?"

"That is none of your business any more than my relationship with anyone is."

Erin glared at him.

"No offence, but as you know, we were supposed to get the paintings after you. Your policeman implied they might have been stolen in Brownsville, which they were not."

"I wouldn't know what he thought or implied."

Surely, if she kept her answers brief, he would take the point and leave.

"Of course since then you have had a couple of murders as well. Any progress?"

"Dan, I've already told you I know nothing about any of it, and I have work to do."

She stood, hoping he would take the hint.

"Hey, I'm passing the time of day. Don't get all huffy. I gotta go, anyway."

"Good-bye, then."

"Yeah, no hard feelings?"

"Of course not."

And good riddance, she thought as the door slammed behind him. What a gossip the man was. And he used too much aftershave.

Chapter Twenty

Kyle was dreaming about his mother, not as he last saw her, her face bruised and bleeding, but happy and smiling, making him breakfast. In his dream, it was summer and sunshine filled the shabby kitchen. As he woke, the dream faded, but the smell of bacon and toast lingered. Then he remembered:

"Come in here."

The two little boys, frightened and hopeful, followed the woman into the house. It was as though they had stepped into a magical land. Paintings of flowers, birds, butterflies and all kinds of fanciful animals covered the walls, the chairs, even the floor. A table in one corner held a collection of paints. A chair in front of it sat before an easel.

"Come in here and take off those wet clothes."

She belonged in a magic land, too. She was the tallest woman Kyle had ever seen. Her grey hair hung in long braids over her dress or nightgown or something. She gave each of them a shirt to wear and put their wet clothes and them, near the stove.

She sat smoking a little black cigar while the boys attacked sandwiches and hot chocolate. When they had finished eating and had begun to look more like little boys and less like small, frightened animals, she asked, "Who are you?"

"I'm Kyle Bassett, and this is my brother, Mike."

"Bassett? Who's your father?"

"Gord Bassett."

"The one who owns the cabin along the lake here?"

"Yes."

"I heard shots over there. What's going on?"

Kyle reluctantly told her the story.

"Kyle, you can't keep running away. By now the police will have called in the search and rescue to try and find you. I want you boys to go to sleep, and in the morning, we'll go talk to them."

"Will you stay with us?"

Kyle desperately wanted to trust this lady.

"Yes. In the morning we'll talk about it. You go to sleep now."

The woman heard the boys stirring and took them their clothes.

"You boys get up and wash your hands and faces. Breakfast is almost ready."

Bacon and eggs and toast and juice and milk and jam. Kyle hadn't had a good breakfast for a long time. Mostly his mother was too sore or too sad to get out of bed.

"Who are you?" he asked when he had finished mopping the last evidence of egg from his plate.

"I'm your Aunt Tabby, your father's half-sister. We had different fathers, so my name is Tabitha Young. We inherited these acres from our mother's father. I never knew your father well; I lived with my mother, and he lived with his father. I didn't know you were all having such a hard time with him."

"Does he know you're here? Maybe he'll come here. We have to run away. By now he's mad at us. He has no one left to hit, only us."

"I won't let anything bad happen to you. We'll go to the police and find out about your mother. Don't cry, Mike."

She put her arm around the whimpering younger boy.

"You're safe with me."

Kyle watched as his new aunt cleaned up the dishes and tidied her cabin.

"Do you live here all the time?"

"Most of the time. I have a house in Culver's Mills, but I like to paint out here. Your father never told you that you had some more family?"

"No. I don't think Mom knows about you either."

"I'm sure she doesn't. Your father and I have only met each other a few times, and we don't like each other. You come on now, use the outhouse, and we'll drive over to your dad's cabin."

After a visit to the little building they had run into in the dark, they went into another shed they hadn't noticed. The longest, pinkest car Kyle had ever seen sat behind the doors.

"Aunt Tabby, what kind of car is this?"

"A Cadillac. I've had it since it was new."

The two boys climbed into the rear seat, slipping and sliding over the black leather, trying to keep the big dog on the floor between them.

Tabitha maneuvered the car out of the clearing, down the narrow lane and out onto the dirt road that led to her brother's cabin. They could see the helicopter hovering over the woods as they drove.

"The cops are going to be so mad at us," Kyle said.

"No, they aren't. But they'll have to ask you what you saw."

"I won't get Dad in trouble."

"Think about your mother, Kyle. They need to know what happened to her."

The big Caddy nosed into the lane behind the long line of police vehicles. When the boys got out of the car, leaving their dog behind, two alert noses sniffed the air, and then the dogs bayed and dragged their handlers towards the boys.

The searchers froze into mug-shot poses, all staring at the tall, grey-haired woman and the two little boys who stood close to her.

"Who is Lieutenant Davidson?"

"I am," said Adam as he walked across the clearing towards her. "Who are you?"

"Tabitha Young. These boys are the ones you're looking for, and they're my nephews."

"How long have they been with you?"

"Since last night and before you ask, I have no phone. They were exhausted and needed rest and food."

"We need to talk to them, ma'am."

"Yes, you do, but not here. They're frightened and worried about their mother. I propose to take them to my house in town. You're welcome to come and speak to them there. Follow us in if you like."

"Kyle, do you and Mike want to stay with your aunt?" Adam said when she paused for breath.

"Yes, until Mom is better. Is she in the hospital?"

"Yes. Your sister is with her. Okay, Ms. Young, I'll follow you in."

Adam heard the fear in Kyle's voice when he asked about his mother and saw how he clung to the woman. Best to see him away from all the uniforms and that cabin.

Chapter Twenty-One

Today, thought Anne, as she huddled deeper under the pile of quilts. Today, she would try to draw the mill. With that, she got up and dressed, and followed the morning smells of coffee and bacon to the kitchen. She dropped her sketchbook and pencil case on the table and sank into the nearest chair. She watched the hummingbirds at the feeder in their aerial battles.

"Are you going to draw something?" Catherine asked. "I didn't know you sketched."

"It's a new hobby for me. My mother was an artist and one day she assured me I could draw and brought out a sketchbook and pencil and got me started. I'm a bit more serious about it and took some classes last winter."

"Where are you going today?"

"Down to the mill. I want to draw the scaffolding against the stone, with early morning shadows. I haven't done any drawing in public before, so I hope there aren't too many people around."

She sat on a bench in the chilly early morning, watching the mist rise from the weir. The stone wall that bordered the river braced her feet and her knees propped up her sketchbook as she drew. The bridge, the weir and the old mill formed an attractive composition.

Anne took several photographs so she could continue to work when she went home, but now she drew sketch after sketch, trying to get the relationships and mass of the building before the light changed.

Sketching silenced her thoughts as she concentrated on getting the shapes and shadows in front of her down on paper. She often wished she had known while she was still practicing medicine. Even gardening left plenty of room for worry and the pain of her husband's loss.

She didn't hear Catherine park the car behind her, walk over and sit down on the other end of the bench. Anne was rubbing her drawing with an eraser.

"Problems?" Catherine asked.

"Oh, no. The eraser is my best tool. I need to put down an incorrect line before I can see where the correct one should go."

"Is this your final drawing?"

"No. I'll finish from my sketches and photos. Thanks."

Catherine handed her a mug and a paper bag. "Mmm, muffins too. I was getting a bit hungry."

"Anyone by to speak to you?"

"Not so far. Not even a jogger. It's early, yet."

"Did you enjoy your dinner with Erin?"

"Yes, she's a lovely person. An odd thing happened, though."

"What?"

"When I was in the washroom, I overheard Mary having a conversation with someone, all about a mysterious offer for Evan's. For 300 thousand dollars, no less. Mary seemed to think that was far more than it was worth."

"Yes. Who was she talking to?"

"Mary came out, but I never did see anyone else. She came over to us and asked about our meal and so on. I suppose the other person went into the kitchen. I didn't recognize the voice."

"Did Erin say if the police were any closer to finding out who killed the man?"

"Oh, she didn't say. Those two little boys are still missing in the bush, she said."

"I bet she didn't say 'the bush'."

Catherine laughed at Anne's Canadian use of the word that expressed not only forest but the remote country to the north.

"No, I think she said woods. Another strange thing. A fire broke out, but Matilde discovered it and called the fire department before it got out of control. The dog didn't bark."

"Maybe it was an accident."

"The fire department thought arson, so why didn't the dog bark? This all revolves around Evan's: the pictures, Trevelyan's claims, the offer for the place, the fire. Do you know anything about Mary and Andre?"

"No, they're newcomers, three years or so."

Anne and Catherine hadn't noticed a walker who crept up behind them. Both jumped when she said hello.

"I'm sorry to startle you," she said. "I was interested in your drawing. I'm Janice Maynard by the way. I don't think we've met."

"I'm Catherine LaPorte, and the one with the dirty fingers is Anne McPhail," said Catherine, a bit astonished at the picture the other woman presented.

Janice's wild orange hair framed an elaborately (for early morning) made up face. She had been strolling the town wearing a paisley caftan, orange again and lavender. Purple sneakers peeked out beneath the hem.

"I'm sorry I can't offer you coffee."

"Thanks for the thought, but I make a morning trek out to Tim's before I open the shop. Odyssey Travel?"

"Oh, yes. I've enjoyed the displays in your front window. Not that travel is on my horizon."

"Too bad. I must be off," Janice said, turning to continue her colorful progress across the bridge.

"What's the matter?" Catherine said.

"Do you think she was listening to us? I didn't hear her walk up."

"Does it matter?"

"I'd like to know how much she overheard. Who is she?"

"Another newcomer. Her agency opened three years ago, at about the same time as Evans. Is there anything else about her?"

"No, but she makes me uneasy. I think I'll pack up, now."

Anne stuffed her sketch pad and pencil away in her backpack.

"I would like to see inside the mill someday."

"Oh, I can arrange that. When?"

"Tomorrow?"

"Sure."

Anne's thoughts tumbled around Evan's and Trevelyan. Why would anyone want the old house so much? Restaurants didn't make much money, and the land was just a lot in town, surrounded by single-family homes and an occasional multi-unit building. She hadn't heard of any development plans, and neither had Catherine. She should ask Peg.

Trevelyan wanted the house the way a child wants a toy because he thought it was his. It might be his. She had seen wills and traced the ownership down through the generations. Perhaps other cousins had an equal claim. She would ask Adam to let her see his papers again. She wondered if the contents went with the house, perhaps something valuable.

"Anne, are you with me? Do you want to go home now or do you have something else to do?"

"Oh, I'm sorry. I was thinking. I'm going to drop in at the station and have lunch at Lil's. Thank you for the snack."

Catherine left, and Anne continued towards the square and the police station. She met Adam in the parking lot and heard the news about the boys.

"Adam," Anne said as she paced his office. "This doesn't make sense to me. I don't understand why, if this guy who was killed was an international art thief—you did say international?"

Adam nodded, and she went on. "Why was he bothering with such a little job. A hundred thousand at most. Why would someone make an outrageous offer for Evan's? That was three times what the pictures were worth. And killing for that."

Anne paused for breath and Adam took the opportunity to say, "Slow down and try to sit down. We'll find them and the answers. Are you afraid, they, whoever they are, will attack you again?"

"No, not really. Well, yes, some." Anne sat. "Mr. Trevelyan is almost dead, and that poor woman is in the hospital, and now her children are homeless. I can't stop thinking and trying to understand. What if the pictures are clues to something else or if something is hidden in them?"

"Hidden in them?"

"A more valuable painting underneath?"

"The curator would have noticed a fake. She's a sharp lady. Everything you mentioned is possible, but there isn't anything to suggest any of them."

"Why did Bassett run? Do you think it was because of the attack on Trevelyan?"

"He did assault his wife, and we don't know for sure he was involved at the library. I'm going to talk to his kids."

"You mean question them about their dad's activities?"

Anne was appalled.

"Yes."

"They must be traumatized."

"I don't know. They're with their aunt."

Adam went on to tell Anne about Tabitha Young.

"How is their mother?"

"Bad. She's going to need reconstructive surgery, and the doctor is afraid she's suffered major brain damage.

"I bet Bassett didn't hit me."

"Why?"

"If he hit his wife like that, I think he would have hit me that hard too, and I would be dead. It wasn't that strong a blow."

"You were out."

"Yes, but I had two head injuries the last time I was in this town. These things add up."

"Someone less vicious?"

"Or not so strong. A woman?"

"A woman? Do you have anyone in mind?"

"It was the strange reaction I had at the antique show."

"What was it?"

"A sort of flashback to the event. It was triggered by a smell. Someone's perfume, I think."

"Did you recognize anyone?"

"By the time I looked around, there was no one near me I recognized."

"Tell me if it happens again."

"Will the little boys receive some therapy? How old are they?"

"Ten and eleven. They're tough kids, bullies at school."

"All the more reason. A therapist might be able to interrupt the cycle of violent behavior. Will you mention it to their aunt?"

"Sure."

"Could I have my papers and computer? I want to dig further into Mr. Trevelyan's genealogy. Perhaps, there are other relatives with a claim. His work didn't mention any cousins, but you never know."

"Okay."

After she left, Adam sat for a while staring at a list of women's names associated with the case. Some, like Erin, he crossed off. Others, like Andrew's wife he put a question mark beside. Time to talk to those kids, he thought. He didn't notice the small car that followed him out of the station parking lot.

Tabitha's old Victorian house stood back from the street, the foundation shrubs hidden by a lawn-full of tall weeds. Paint curled on the window sills and peeled from the once-white columns of the front porch. The windows shone though, and the front walk was swept clear. Not house- proud, but clean, Adam guessed.

The interior confirmed his impression. Piles of books, stacks of canvases and old magazines filled every corner of the living room. No dust. The boys' wary eyes followed him as he walked across to an armchair near where they sat close together, playing some electronic game.

"How ya doin' guys?"

"Okay," said Kyle, while Mike huddled back behind his brother.

Tabitha sat down on the couch, a little distant, but close enough to reassure the boys they weren't alone.

"Kyle, you're the oldest. Can you tell me what happened at your house?"

"I don't want to get my dad in trouble."

"Kyle, I told you the truth will help now," Tabitha said.

"Mom and Dad had a fight."

"What happened?"

"Dad hit her, and she fell down."

"And then he kicked her, and her mouth was bleeding, and she didn't get up."

"Then he took us to Grandma's old house and then out to the camp," Kyle said.

"Where is Grandma's old house?"

"In the country."

"Which Grandma, Kyle? Grandma Bassett?" Tabitha asked.

"Yes."

"It's out the Grass Lake Road," Tabitha told Adam. "It's been derelict for years."

"Why did you go there? Do you know, Kyle?"

"Dad had some stuff to put there. He keeps stuff in the house. Can we see our mom?"

"I want to see Chrissy," Mike said.

"Why? You know she hates us. She hates Dad, and she hates us."

"I want to. She helps me when I have bad dreams."

"Did you have a bad dream last night?" Adam asked.

"Yes, I have lots of them."

"He talks in his sleep, too. Do we have to talk any more?"

"No. Thanks, fellows."

Adam shook hands with each child and shrugged his head towards the door, asking Tabitha to follow him. "I think you need to get these kids some therapy. Can you do that?"

"Yes, I can."

Adam turned at the intersection and a small blue-grey car, a Honda passed him. Adam hadn't noticed anything more about the driver except he was male and slight.

The Honda parked in Tabitha's driveway where the driver sat for a moment watching the street behind him. Convinced the policeman hadn't followed, he got out and up the porch stairs to ring the doorbell.

"Yes?" Tabitha said.

"I need to talk to the boys."

"Certainly not. Who are you?"

"Someone with a gun aimed at you. Open the door."

Tabitha backed away as he followed her down the hall to the living room. The boys looked up from their play. Only Kyle saw the gun.

"Aunt Tabby, what's he doing?"

"Kid, where's your dad?"

"The cops lost him on the lake."

"Where'd he put the stuff?"

"What stuff?"

"Don't be smart, or your aunt here will get hurt. Where'd he take the big box?"

"To the old Bassett house on Grass Lake Road."

"Aunt Tabby, no."

"Whatever it is, it isn't worth our lives, Kyle."

"Now get out of my house."

"Did the kid tell the cop?"

"Yes."

At that, the slight man turned and left after uttering one profane word.

"Aunt Tabby, now he'll take Dad's stuff. Dad'll be even madder at us," said Mike.

Tabitha wasn't listening. She dialed the police and left a message for Adam.

Chapter Twenty-Two

Hungry customers filled the stools and booths of the diner, but Erin saw Anne come in and waved to her from the tiny two-person table she occupied at the back of the restaurant.

"Hi, Anne. Join me. There isn't breathing room anywhere else."

"Thanks. I'll tell Peg what I want."

Western sandwich and fries had been Anne's weakness since university. She still remembered Sunday mornings in the Student's Union, studying and breakfast with her boyfriend. Peg's version took her back to those days.

She slid into the booth, and Erin asked if she felt better.

"Oh, much, thanks."

"What are you up to now?"

"Sketching. I attempted the old mill this morning."

"May I see?"

"Sure, but I warn you, I'm a beginner."

Anne took the big sketch pad from her backpack and handed it to Erin.

"Yes, you are, but you have a good strong line, the perspective is excellent, and you are beginning to be able to suggest volume and texture. I say keep at it. You do enjoy it?"

"Oh, yes. Thanks for the input. Catherine is going to take me inside the mill tomorrow. I've been in one other old mill, but it was a different type, wood, not stone, and it was a sawmill, not a gristmill. I understand this one is to be renovated and put to alternative use?"

"Yes, a theatre, workshop, gallery and restaurant complex."

"Perhaps it will help increase tourism here."

"That's the idea."

"Would you move?"

"No. The square is already on the must-see list, so I'll stay here."

"I was at the courthouse. Did you know the little boys have been found?"

"Peg told me. That's wonderful. I'm sure Adam will be so relieved. What did they do with the boys?"

"They are going to stay with their aunt, an artist called Tabitha Young. I think all this is connected: the library thefts, the murder, the attacks on Mr. Trevelyan and me—too much crime for one little place in too short a time. I think something, some piece of the puzzle is missing."

"Missing?"

"Yes. An additional motive. Something worth a lot more money than that Belknap would bring."

"Yes, I agree. The Belknap and the sampler together would be one hundred thousand maximum and likely a lot less."

"The dead man was an art thief. I wonder what type of works he stole and if anything similar is missing here. Is his wife still here?"

"I think she's the woman sitting in the window seat."

Erin nodded towards the other end of the diner where Alisse Bertrand sat, pushing food around on her plate and staring out at the fall day.

"What are you thinking?"

"Couldn't you hide a more valuable painting behind another?"

"Not in a modern frame."

"The frames of the Belknap and the sampler would be old."

"Maybe but aren't you inventing a crime and a criminal if you think his widow is waiting around to get the goods?"

"I suppose so. No data, you mean."

"Yes, no data."

Their food had arrived, and conversation stopped. The customer in the booth behind them got up, leaving a bill on the table and a scent in the air.

As the scent reached Anne, she felt a sudden rush of nausea and clutched the table. As soon as she could, she looked around but saw only the closing door. Everyone in the diner was familiar to her from previous visits. Alisse Bertrand was gone.

"Anne, what's the matter?"

She reached across the table to touch Anne's hand.

"It's a flashback thing that's been happening to me. When I smell a particular fragrance, I get nauseated and panic. The last time I flashed back to the assault at Trevelyan's. Did you notice a woman sitting behind me? Did the Bertrand woman come over near here?"

"No, I didn't. I saw Dan Abbott earlier, but no one else."

"As soon as I can travel, I'm going home. Maybe the day after tomorrow, the doctor said."

"That's too bad. You were looking forward to a pleasant holiday, this year."

"Yes, I was. I hope life will be more peaceful in Bermuda next month."

"You're going to Bermuda, too? Adam and I are going as well next month."

"Yes, I'm going to visit my sister and her family."

"Have you been before? Can you tell me something about it?"

"Sure."

The conversation wandered into what to eat, where to stay, and what to see on the little island Anne loved.

Erin's seat overlooked the square.

"That's odd," she said, interrupting Anne's description of the Bermuda Art Gallery.

"The Gallery isn't odd."

"No, what Adam did was odd. He was driving along the square toward the courthouse, but when he got to the corner, he accelerated and took the road north, fast."

"Must have had a call."

"I guess. Do you have plans for the afternoon?"

"I'm going to do some shopping, and I have an appointment to meet with Ted Atkins. I usually don't talk to the press, but I owe him. He saved my life last year, you remember?"

"Yes. But doing that saved him too. He had been so depressed since he lost his wife and daughters in a terrible crash. After he saved you, he stopped drinking and started living again."

She leaned closer to whisper, "And he's seeing Peg."

"Is he? I thought she was looking better because of the money."

"Oh, no. By the way, did you tell Adam you were going to talk to Ted?"

"No. I won't say anything specific to Ted. I'd better go if I'm going to make the appointment. See you later."

She walked back to Catherine's, enjoying the autumn sunshine. Someone somewhere was burning leaves, and the lovely, acrid scent drifted over the town.

Chapter Twenty-Three

Ted Atkins lounged across from the diner, watching the activity around the square and the elegant car parked in front of Lil's. He saw Anne go in for lunch, watched Adam accelerate out of the square, but kept his eye on the Porsche. A story from the widow might be worthwhile for the Saturday paper if he could get her to talk.

Alisse lingered in her window seat for a few minutes after her lunch, twiddling with a spoon and staring out the window. Finally, she left, drawing curious glances and leaving a wake of furtive whispers as she walked the length of the diner as smoothly as though she were on a runway in Paris.

The engine of Ted's car protested twice before it turned over and caught. He moved out to follow Alisse as she took the northwest exit from the square. No need to follow too closely, he thought. Taking this route, she was likely going back to the inn where she had been staying since she had arrived in town. He didn't notice the truck that followed him as he turned onto the county road.

The Inn on the Shore had taken over the property of a nineteenth-century estate, whose lovely gardens opened onto the shore of Lake Champlain. Although built as a farmhouse, the house had been enlarged over the years and now had an enviable reputation for its cuisine and comfort. Alisse parked her car behind the inn under the shade of an outbuilding that had sheltered carriages and weary horses in days past. Her heels clicked on the bricks of the courtyard. The door of the inn escaped her nervous fingers and slammed shut. The woman dusting in the hallway looked up in surprise.

"Oh, I am sorry to have disturbed you."

Alisse swept past on her way up the stairs, not looking at the other woman.

Once she was inside her room, tears coursed down in black rivulets over the elegant cheekbones. Alisse let them come. She had loved John, criminal though he might have been. The thought of his imagined infidelity had made her want to leave him. Now she felt the vast space his death left in her life. She wanted to go home, but they hadn't released him to her, and she wasn't going to leave him here alone.

As the tears subsided, she thought about arrangements she had to make. Perhaps the Inn could recommend a local funeral home to help her.

The jangle of the phone startled her. Not the police again, she thought, for who else would call her here.

"Mrs. Bertrand, a visitor for you. His name is Ted Atkins."

"What does he want?"

"He didn't say."

"A moment."

Anything to distract her, she thought.

Ted hadn't known what an astonishingly beautiful woman she was.

As she floated down the stairs, he stood up, straightening his tie, and passing a hand over his unruly hair.

"Mrs. Bertrand, thanks for seeing me. I'm Ted Atkins with the Culver's Mills Watchman.

"I didn't realize you were the press. I have no comment. Please leave me in peace."

"Did you know the local TV station is suggesting, not so subtly, that you were part of your husband's gang and that your arrest is imminent and that is why you're still here."

"That is not true."

Her face paled, and her lovely mouth drew into a thin line.

"Maybe we should go outside," Ted suggested with a glance at the woman who lingered nearby, dusting the objects in the sitting room.

"Very well."

They walked across the parking area and onto a brick path, through the garden, across a meadow and down to a bench where the grass and flowers fell away to sand and the water. Seagulls swooped in their aerial dance, their raucous calls punctuating the beauty of their flight.

They sat in silence for a few minutes.

"It takes a while, but the pain goes away a little, and you can breathe again."

"You have lost someone also?"

"My wife and child."

"Both."

She turned to him, her eyes brimming over.

"I am so sorry."

"It was bad for a long time, but now I've met someone, and life is starting to be good again.

"Perhaps your wife was not a thief?"

"No, but does the fact he was a thief change your feelings for him?"

"Non, non," her voice trailed away as she turned to the lake again.

Ted leaned forward, gripping his hands between his knees. A piece of the bench tore away, and a bullet hit the sand beside his feet. Screaming filled the air, but he couldn't tell if it was Alisse or the seagulls, as he dragged her onto the sand and behind a hillock that offered a little protection. "Who's shooting at us?"

She clutched at Ted's coat.

"At you, you mean."

"At me?"

"Someone thinks you know something. Keep your head down."

He pushed her head into the sand as another bullet pounded into the beach. He reached 911, shouting his location to the operator. More shots. He dragged Alisse along the sand crawling behind the meagre cover of the eroded shoreline. The sound of the shots had brought people out of the Inn and the barns. Yelling voices mixed with the roar of a vehicle somewhere close. Quiet, and then the calls were for Allise. They lay on the sand for long moments waiting for the callers to reach them, reluctant to leave the safety of the little hill of grass and sand. The distant wail of a siren assured them of rescue.

Ted cautiously raised his head as the concierge from the inn appeared beside the bench.

"Are you all right?" she asked.

"No," Allise whispered.

Fear twisted the lovely features, turned into a mask by the clinging sand. Blood dripped from her arm, staining the soft cream of her shirt. Her body slumped, and he caught her and supported her up and over the edge of the meadow and onto the path. Workers from the inn crowded the path. Beyond them, Ted could see police cars arriving.

"Why does someone want to kill me?" Alisse whimpered.

"Your husband's partners, tying up loose ends."

"I don't know anything."

"They don't know that."

An ambulance had arrived, and Ted stood nearby as the paramedics bandaged the wound in Alisse's arm. He phoned a quick report to the paper and called for a photographer. After the crew left with Alisse, he spoke to the county police and drove to town. He had an appointment to talk to Anne McPhail.

"Hi," Ted called, as he climbed out of his dilapidated car. Anne was sitting on the porch. "Would you like to go somewhere for a coffee to do this?"

"Sure, let's go to Tim's."

They took their drinks and Ted's cruller to a table in the corner. Ted told Anne more details of the shooting at the Inn.

"Will she be all right?" Anne asked.

"I think so. The bullet hit her shoulder, but she was breathing okay."

"Afterwards is hardest. I still dream about last year. That's why I am worried about those two little boys. Such a terrible experience may lead to post-traumatic stress syndrome. They need some counseling."

Anne was careful to avoid any mention of the work she was doing for Adam but did tell Ted more about the syndrome she had mentioned and suggested the boys needed a stable and compassionate home to recover from their ordeal.

Chapter Twenty-Four

The office patched Tabitha's call to Adam as he reached the square. Calling Pete to meet him, he took the Grass Lake Road towards the old house the boys described. When he closed on the blue Honda, he switched on his siren, but the little car ahead accelerated, disappearing into a tight s-curve to the right the road took before it reached the old Bassett house. Too fast, Adam thought.

The driver lost control at the right turn. The car arced off the hill hit a stand of old pine growing out of a mound of rock, flipped, and caught fire. A plume of black smoke rose from the burning car. He put through the call for the emergency crew.

He slid down the embankment, but couldn't get close to the burning car. His eyes and throat burned from the dense smoke that shrouded the car and its driver.

Dammit, where was that fire truck? Two minutes passed. A siren sounded in the distance. Police. A cruiser skidded to a stop.

"Adam, get the hell up here. The car's gonna blow again."

Adam turned toward Pete's frantic voice and scrambled up the hill. A blast of heat and sound reached them.

"Christ, Adam, what were you doing?"

"I couldn't reach him."

"Good. You'd be dead now too."

Only the roar and crackle of the fire broke the silence. Five more minutes passed before the fire-trucks arrived.

The firefighter interrupted the flow of Adam's tirade.

"Sorry, Lieutenant. We were at a barn fire the other side of Culver's. We came as quick as we could."

"Yeah, I'm sorry, too. It was over from the time he left the road."

"Who is it?"

"I don't know yet."

The firefighters sprayed foam onto the burning car. They talked to the county police who answered the call.

"We still going out to the old Bassett property?" Pete asked.

"Yeah."

Grandma Bassett's property copied her son's. Car parts and broken vehicles filled most of the yard. In front, the ghosts of garden beds ringed by half-buried tires suggested someone cared a little, likely the grandmother.

"Are we going in?" Pete asked.

"Not now. With the guy dead, we can wait for a warrant. I want you to stay here while I speak to the judge. If Bassett shows up, call for backup if you can before arresting him. I'll be back in half-an-hour or so."

"I dealt with him before."

"Yeah, but take the shotgun."

Before Adam left for town, they circled the house and barn, looking for signs of recent activity. Nothing. Pete settled into a weathered rocker on the shabby front porch, his shotgun across his knees, as he watched Adam leave.

Adam was back in less than the promised half hour. As he drove up, he took a closer look at the property. Clapboard once painted white, now aged to grey, covered the two stories. Weathered black shutters outlined most of the windows. No broken glass, though. The porch hung from the front of the house, propped at each end by a stack of concrete blocks. The front door was a surprise—new and fitted with an expensive lock.

"Want me to take out the lock with the shotgun?"

"No, let's try the back first. These locks are expensive. Maybe they went for a cheaper model for the kitchen door."

The back door was as fortified as the front, but a kitchen window wasn't. Pete climbed through and let Adam in.

Stacks of boxes, most containing electronics, competed for space with the few remaining pieces of furniture. It was going to take a week to inventory the stuff, Adam thought.

"There's a sort of office in here with a computer. Want me to see what's on it?" said Pete.

"Sure. Find me a list of suppliers."

Upstairs he found a room also fitted with a new door. Not locked though. The hum of some equipment came through.

Inside, the humidity control unit sang away to itself. A corner held a pile of the thin, oblong, packing cases like those in the library in Brownsville. Empty. Whatever was in the room to justify its expense was long gone. Paintings, he thought. Andrews was an art thief. Was the accident victim an accomplice? But who cleaned out the room? Someone who wanted the pictures, he guessed but not the electronics. Not too portable.

"Pete," he called, "we need a crew to work this place for evidence. Call it in."

"Okay. Nothing down here. I couldn't find anything on the computer, but Brad might be able to recover something. What about the barn? Want me to take a look?"

"Wait for me."

The barn was a drive shed. Two trailers and a pickup truck, all empty, filled the main floor. Pete checked the loft but found nothing.

When the crew had arrived to go over the house and barn, Adam and Pete left them to it and drove back to town, stopping at the accident scene. A tow truck winched the burned-out car up the slope. The car was stolen in Burlington two days before. Identification of the dead man was going to take some time unless Tabitha Young had a decent description for him.

Tabitha had a surprise for Adam, not a description, a portrait. She had drawn a careful sketch. The small head with its ears tight to it, slicked-back hair and small chin belonged to Dan Abbott, the Brownsville librarian. Another criminal librarian. What went on in those places? Adam thanked Tabitha and headed back to the station.

Now Adam had three: Bassett, Abbott and Andrews.

Someone else had the art.

The media, represented by Ted Atkins, one TV reporter with a cameraman, and a young woman who free-lanced for the major Burlington paper, met Adam at the steps of the courthouse.

"Nothing at the moment, ladies and gentlemen."

Adam strode by and on up the steps, closing off their protests with the heavy oak door. What the hell had happened?

"What's going on, Brad?"

Brad jumped to follow Adam into his office, closing the door behind him.

"A shooter out at the Inn on the Lake. Ted Atkins was out there interviewing Alisse Bertrand. They were sitting down by the lake when bullets flew by. The first one missed them, but the second one caught her in the shoulder. She's at the hospital. The sheriff let Atkins go, and he hasn't been back to his paper yet."

"He's outside the door. Go get him."

Pallor and fatigue marked Ted's face as he came in and collapsed on one of the hard-backed chairs in Adam's office. He passed his hand over his head and settled back.

"What the hell's happening, Adam?"

"You tell me. Why is someone trying to kill you? Where have you been poking around?"

Ted gripped the arms as he leaned forward in his chair.

"Whoever it was, was shooting at her, not me."

"Was anyone following her out there?"

"No, I didn't notice a damn thing until the shot hit the seat behind me, and then all I could think of was getting her down and getting behind something."

"What did you hear?"

"Hear? Nothing."

Ted frowned and rubbed his hand over his face again.

"Something?"

"Maybe a truck, a big engine, taking off."

"Do you think she's in it?"

"No."

"What have you been doing?"

"Not much. Talking to people about Bassett."

"Anything out of the ordinary?"

"He might have been taking a trip. He's been in and out of the travel agent—the woman with the wigs—a couple of times. That's about all. I have to file, Adam, so if you have nothing else?"

Ted stood up and moved towards the door.

"You remember anything, you call me. Don't wait to publish. And watch your back."

Ted waved a hand at him as he closed the door.

"Sure."

Brad had tapped a chart of the investigation to the wall of Adam's office. Adam added the shooting, with a tentative link to the travel agent. Dying rays from the sun stained the chart a vivid red for a few minutes.

"I'm going, boss," Brad called.

Adam called the hospital, hoping to be able to interview Alisse, but she had been airlifted to Burlington for surgery on her shoulder. He would have to see her when he went down to his law class.

Chapter Twenty-Five

Anne snuggled under the quilts, allowing the chill morning air to catch the tip of her nose. Winter was surely coming, though the sky she glimpsed through the branches outside her promised a bright day. It's the end of September, she thought. No snow yet.

She threw off the covers. Today, she and Catherine were going to visit the old mill, and Catherine said earlier would be better. There were still tourists in town.

An eighteenth-century gristmill consists of three parts, read the information posted at the entrance. An outer freestanding structure rests on its foundation while an inner building houses the milling equipment. The water works, comprising a wheel, dam, millrace and pond, lie outside the two. The outer and inner walls don't connect, preventing wear and tear on the outer building. A stairwell leads from the entrance floor to the main floor. The exterior wall is punctuated by windows.

On the ground level, a large door opened to allow delivery of grain. An interior catwalk ran along three sides, overlooking the works. Ancient chestnut, impervious to insects and rot, joined granite from local quarries as the building's materials.

Anne and Catherine climbed the wide staircase to the level of the catwalk. Little of the works remained. Below stood the ancient stones that had provided the area with flour. Shafts of light from high windows, glittering with dust, bounced off the metal remains below. Shadows created mysterious shapes and suggested hidden forms.

"How will they convert it? Are they planning any restoration or preservation?"

Anne's voice echoed back across the mill works.

"They plan to preserve a working water-wheel for the sound effect and interest and the exterior. Otherwise, no. I haven't seen any working drawings, but I know plans include an art gallery up here and a theatre. Possibly a small restaurant and patio, by the business office, will be added. I know an extensive garden is planned. There has been some opposition."

"From whom?"

"Old mill enthusiasts. They'd like it restored as a working mill and museum."

"Is that a possibility?"

"Much more expensive, and there are many of them in Vermont and other parts of New England."

As they walked along, Anne noticed some words carved in the floor. As she bent over to read them, an explosion of sound filled the old building. A bullet buried itself in the timber above her.

"Down," she yelled at Catherine.

But Catherine was lying beside her, behind the low wall.

"Move, move, so he doesn't know where we are."

Hands and knees propelled them down the catwalk. Another bullet, this one hitting the wall behind them.

"There's a window. Do they open?" Anne said.

"Yes, from the bottom."

"What's outside this wall?"

"The millpond."

"Can you swim? Is it deep?"

"Yes."

Another bullet, further away. He was firing into the wall at steady intervals, moving away from them, towards the open door.

They reached the window. If the latch stuck or screeched, he would find them.

"Be ready to go fast when I push out. He might hear it."

There was little noise from the latch itself, but a tentative push at the window brought an ominous groan. They would only have a few seconds.

"Ready?"

"Yes."

Anne pushed; the window gave; rotting hinges screeched a protest.

"Go."

Catherine jumped. A bullet splintered the window frame. Anne couldn't stand to jump; he would see her. She turned and slipped over, hanging from the edge. How she hated heights. She pushed away and plummeted into the black water below.

Deep, she thought, Catherine said it was deep. She held her breath as she went down and closed her eyes. She hit the water straight, her knees up in the cannonball she learned jumping into the Madawaska River at home. She opened her eyes to black-green water. A random memory of herself at twelve, the river, a perfect summer day, the water the same color with the sun shining through.

At least she hadn't hit Catherine. She surfaced facing the building. A figure filled the window.

She dove and swam, straight down the pond as far as she could, came up, gasped air, and dove again. Now she was nearer to a bank. After one more dive, she surfaced at the bank, with overhanging branches between her and the shooter.

No one in the window. Did that mean he knew where she was? She had to move again. Which way? Where was he? Watching from another spot? Adrenaline fuelled her escape, but her energy was draining away; she was cold, and her drenched clothes weighed her down.

She had to climb out and hide.

Anne crawled up the bank and into a dense thicket. She listened and shivered for long minutes. Nothing. No sirens either. What happened to Catherine? Maybe the shooter was after her? What if the guy from Brownsville was crazier than she thought?

She tried to remember what surrounded the pond. A park, she thought, most of it natural, so there was cover. Yes, for the shooter too, she reminded herself. Jogging and bicycle paths. People, she thought with relief, even this early.

She crept to the edge of her lovely safe thicket and realized she was a few feet from the path.

A figure in flowing scarlet made stately progress along the path. It was the strange woman from the travel agency, she thought. Should she call her? No, she listened to Catherine and her talk about the murder. Could she be part of this? The caftan she wore could conceal a gun.

Anne edged back, deeper into the bushes. Sirens wailed, and tires squealed. They were here. She would hide until they came close to her.

When Catherine hit the water, her one thought was to get out. She knew the pond well from swimming with her boys. At the corner of the mill, underwater steps rose to the surface and on to the grass. The water spilled over the wheel there.

The steps were slick with algae. Catherine fell, gashing her knee. She lay panting at the top of the stairs for a moment and then she heard another shot. He was still upstairs. She raced across the park to the street where her friend Zoe lived, two houses away. She pounded on the back door.

Catherine fell against the doorjamb when Zoe opened the door. "Call the police. Someone is shooting at Anne at the mill," She sank to the floor and leaned back, panting.

* * *

Brad took the call. The squad room emptied as he, Pete, Dave and Adam ran for their vehicles. The two-minute drive to the mill went by in slow motion for Adam, as he remembered the other times Anne had been attacked and came near to death.

The mill was quiet. No shooting. No body was floating in the millpond.

"Brad, you and Pete take the mill. Dave, come with me. We'll search this side," Adam said.

He spoke into his radio, sending another team along the far bank. How normal it looked. A couple walked with their dog, and the woman from the travel agency sauntered along the path.

* * *

The couple and the dog approached Anne's thicket.with their dog. The dog knew she was there. He nosed into the underbrush. Good. The man dragged the curious dog along the path and away from her hiding spot.

Next to pass was a woman in a long red dress. Searching, Anne thought. Anne ground her face into the dirt and leaves, hoping nothing of her clothes showed through. Long minutes passed.

"Anne."

Someone called her name. Adam, she was sure. She raised her head a fraction and peered along the path. Yes.

"Adam," she whispered as they passed. Then, louder, urgently, she called again. "Adam."

"Where are you?"

"Here, in the bushes. I'm afraid he's watching."

"We'll keep you between us."

Adam helped her up and supported her. Her jeans and shirt, covered with pond scum and dirt, clung to her and she smelled the way they looked.

"Catherine?" Is she?"

"She's fine. She made the call to us."

"Thank God. She wasn't hurt?"

"Split open her knee. She's gone for stitches. We need to talk to you if you are up to it."

"I need a shower first."

"We'll take you home and wait for you."

"Okay. I'm freezing," she said through chattering teeth.

After a long shower and hot toddy, Anne felt warm at last. She sat in Catherine's little front room, petting Maggie who lolled on the ottoman at her feet. Adam sat in the rocker across from her. Back from the hospital, Catherine was recovering in her bed.

"Tell me what happened," Adam asked.

"Catherine and I were walking along the catwalk on the pond side of the building. I bent down to look at something as he fired and the bullet hit the wall behind me. We crawled along to a window and jumped into the pond. He was still firing. Then he shot at me from the window, but he missed me because I swam underwater. The water was so black he couldn't see me, I guess. I crawled out from the pond and hid in the bushes until you came. That's all."

Anne leaned back against her pillow and closed her eyes.

"Did you see him?"

"I saw a silhouette. I say him, but I don't know even that."

"Do you have any idea why?"

"No."

"Have you talked about the case to anyone?"

"Erin and Catherine. I talked to Erin in Lil's and Catherine on the bench across from the Mill. Adam, I have to rest. I feel terrible."

"All right. I'll call you later. I'm leaving Dave outside. If Maggie starts barking, call Dave."

"Yes, I will."

* * *

Adam heard the clock in the courthouse tower strike ten as he returned to the station. Time to talk to the boss. Captain Naismith sat behind his desk, feet propped on an open drawer, while Adam put the case and its problems to him.

Naismith summed up when Adam finished.

"You have the theft of the paintings, likely involving Bassett, Abbott, and Andrews; the attacks on Trevelyan and Anne and now on Alisse Bertrand and Atkins; the attempt to buy Evan's and the fire. This shooting at the mill. Do you make Bassett or Abbott for the shootings?"

"Bassett is too big to be the guy at the hospital. Anne thinks if he hit her, she'd be dead, and I agree with her. Abbott was slight. Pete was trying to place him in Culver's when the attacks occurred, but I took him off to work the mill."

"Could it be one of the women? What about the widow Andrews?"

Adam grinned at the thought of elegant Alisse Bertrand in the role of 'the widow Andrews'.

"She has brains, I think, but she's in hospital in Burlington, so she's clear for the attack on Anne and Catherine."

"You have three violent acts," said Naismith. "The attack on Trevelyan can only relate to Evan's and the paintings; the death of Andrews, likely related to the theft; the attack on Anne at the mill."

"Yes. Bassett's gone as far as I can tell. He could have done Andrews and been involved in the theft, but likely not Trevelyan out at the house and not in the hospital. Abbott was dead before the shooting started at the mill. He did have a weapon—we're testing it —and he was slight enough to have been the one at the hospital. Alisse Bertrand is a tall woman, too tall for the hospital job. We don't think she was in the country when her husband was killed. She thinks her husband was having an affair here. She's smart and could have been involved in her husband's illegal business but

"What does the Quebec Surete have to say about her?" Naismith said.

"A well-thought-of artist, no criminal activity in the record."

"Do you have anybody else?"

"Several people around the mill: the woman from the travel agency, and the McDonalds, Al and Bernice, with their dog."

"Who is she, the agent?"

"Her name is Janice Maynard. She set up shop about three years ago. Not part of a chain. Erin and I had her put together our trip to Bermuda, and she seems to know her stuff. I have three little things. Anne thinks Maynard eavesdropped on a conversation she had with Catherine about the case, and she was seen walking near the mill this morning, but she walks every morning. She does wear this long flowing robe that could have concealed a weapon. Atkins says Bassett was in her shop a couple of times."

"Long flowing robes?"

Naismith peered over his glasses at Adam with a quizzical look.

"Yeah, she walks around town in an orange wig and these long, brightly-colored dresses. Erin calls them caftans. She's eccentric, but I have no reason to think she's a criminal."

"Where'd she come from?"

"No clue. I'll get Brad on it."

"Anyone else?"

"No. Anne gets flashbacks when she smells a certain scent, but she hasn't associated it with anyone yet."

"Do you have someone at Catherine's?"

"Yes. The press is outside."

"I'll deal with them."

Anne wanted to review Trevelyan's papers again. Adam sent the file over, hoping something would suggest itself to her.

He spent the rest of the day report writing and following up forensic reports.

By five, he finished his paperwork. Dental records confirmed the dead man was Abbott.

They recovered a gun from the burned-out car, but the tests comparing it to the bullet they found at the motel where Andrews was killed were still pending. Forensic on the bullets and shell casings from the mill were pending.

Adam signed out and drove home to feed Sam and change. Not the best day.

Chapter Twenty-Six

"What are we going to do?"

The whispered voice was taut with fear.

"Relax. No one connects us with this and no one will if you stop trying to kill people. What the hell did you shoot the old guy for? What were you doing?"

"I figured that if they found the picture before we got it back, he would claim it. Maybe he already had it. I wanted to see if he did. He came back and grabbed his shotgun. I had no choice. That woman, that doctor, she's going to figure it out. I heard she solved that case last year and Alisse likely knows something. John couldn't keep his mouth shut in bed."

"No one's going to figure it out. I want you to stop worrying and get rid of your guns."

"No."

"No more killing."

"I want to get out of here."

"If you leave now they'll suspect you. Meet me tonight about 1:00 a.m."

"Where?"

"Down by the river where we met before."

"Where did you hide them?"

"I'll tell you tonight," was the wary reply.

"Okay."

Matilde led Adam and Erin to their table next to the fireplace.

"How was your day?" Erin asked after they ordered their drinks, a bloody Caesar for Adam and Campari and soda for Erin.

"You heard about the mill?"

"No, I wasn't out. What happened?"

"Someone shot at Catherine and Anne. They're both fine."

"Why?"

"I don't know. Someone thinks they know something, I guess. Panic setting in. Someone took a couple of shots at Alisse Bertrand and Ted Atkins too. She's in the hospital with a bullet wound in her shoulder. Anne told me about that strange reaction she's been having. You were with her when one happened?"

"Yes. We were at lunch at Lil's. She got a whiff of perfume and felt dizzy and nauseated. The first time it happened, she told me, she flashed back to the assault."

"Was anyone there?"

"Dan Abbot had left. Nancy Webb, the travel agent, those two lawyers from the office beside Evan's. I can never remember their names."

Adam glanced away from Erin, and she stopped talking as Matilde brought their drinks. She was inclined to loiter, so Adam changed the topic to their upcoming trip.

"Do you still like the idea of a Bed and Breakfast? Some of the hotels have special facilities, spas and so on."

"Oh, I'm looking forward to meeting the people. Large hotels are so impersonal."

"I want you to have the best."

"Remember the picture of that pretty pink house with the verandas up and down and the garden. I'll love it."

"Do you think you will love a moped?"

Bermuda tourists couldn't rent cars, but most attempted the ubiquitous little bikes with the distinctive red license plates that identified them to the local drivers.

"Do they come built for two?"

"I think so," he said.

"Anne told me there is an art gallery in the city hall. She will be in Bermuda at the same time we are, visiting her family."

"I hope she doesn't find any bodies in Bermuda. Do you want to see her there?"

"I doubt she'll have time. She doesn't go for long, and she spends all her time with her family. It's a small place. We might run into her, but Anne and I decided not to plan anything unless you insist?"

"Not me. I want you all to myself."

At that their meals arrived, and the conversation turned, as restaurant conversations do, to the food. Adam was a meat-eater, sticking to old favorites, lamb chops this time. Erin preferred a grilled whitefish accompanied by a surprising number of vegetables.

"Good?" he asked.

"Mmmm."

Towards the end of their meal, Mary, the owner, approached them to ask if all was well.

"Excellent, thank you."

Mary's pleasant face creased into a frown.

"Something bothering you, Mary?"

"I think we've had an intruder."

"What's missing?"

"That's it. Nothing. I found doors ajar that should have been closed, down in the basement for example. I am so nervous after the fire."

"I can send someone over, or come myself tomorrow."

"Would you? I'd appreciate it."

Erin noticed that Mary had waited until Matilde was out of the room to speak to them.

"I don't think she trusts Matilde."

"Neither do I. That woman spends too much time hovering."

"Could be she's a gossip."

After the dessert, they strolled back to Erin's. She had changed the display in the store. She told him furniture of this design had been made mostly in Grand Rapids, in Michigan for the common market, sold through the major catalogue outfits.

Adam leaned back on the sofa, his long legs propped on a footstool. The wooden back and arms of the sofa, ending in lion's head carving, surrounded a new floral-printed fabric. It was high enough and soft enough to be comfortable. An electric fire glowed in a cast-iron fireplace.

They spent most free evenings here or upstairs in her loft. Adam hadn't moved in, but soon, he told himself, soon he would ask her to marry him.

Chapter Twenty-Seven

Anne found herself back under full protection the next day —guard, escort, bulletproof vest and working at the police station, not the library. She wanted to search the Leclerc family tree for any local descendants who might have a claim equal to Trevelyan's. With Trevelyan's research and internet resources, she might be able to construct a complete family tree.

Adam and Pete were discussing the possible break-in at Evan's when Anne and Brad came in.

"I'm going over to talk to Mary and Andre," Adam said. "I want you to find out what you can about the server, Matilde. Brad, you stick with Anne today. I want to know about the Leclercs."

At that, Adam left for the short walk to Evan's.

A north wind blew leaves off trees and into tidy hillocks against the wrought iron fence around the park in the square, where a few scraggly mums still bloomed in the flower beds. Forlorn and chilly pigeons clustered on the lee side of the statue. Cold for this time of year, Adam thought. He hoped it didn't mean an early winter. Cheering himself up with thoughts of sunny Bermuda and Erin, he opened the door of Evan's with a pleasant smile for Mary.

Mary took Adam through into the kitchen of the restaurant.

Chrome and stainless-steel surfaces shone between and above the old oak cupboards. A well-scrubbed pine table filled a bow window overlooking the garden. They sat down to talk.

"I feel a little silly," Mary said, "but I am sure someone has been through this house."

"Have you been away?"

"Yes. We closed for three days to go to a funeral in New York. When we got back, small changes bothered me: drawers open a crack; towels in a different order in my linen cupboard; clothes too close together in my closet. I'm very fussy about those sorts of things."

"Was anything missing?"

"Not that I can see. Would you walk through with me? Perhaps you will notice something I haven't."

"Sure. Your trip to New York was unexpected, then?"

"Yes. Andre's aunt died suddenly. Fortunately, we were able to get away."

The kitchen was in constant use since they returned from the funeral and nothing was out of place.

The dining room told a different story. The glass cabinet on one side of the fireplace, which balanced the inglenook on the other, had been searched, Mary was sure.

He went through the rest of the house, but he found nothing. Even the attics were orderly. Fussy, she said.

A thin layer of dust covered the surfaces in the attic. Even Mary couldn't get up here to clean every day. He followed footprints to one corner in which he saw an impression, a vaguely square shape with blurred edges. He squatted and examined the area. Hadn't he seen this shape before? Crates, he thought, the kind the pictures from the library had been in.

"Did you store boxes up here recently?"

"No. There was nothing in that corner."

"Come and look at this clear space on the floor."

"We didn't have anything there. I haven't been up here for

several months, and Andre almost never does. What do you think it means?"

"It means someone who has access to your home stored something up here."

"Access to the house? Us, Matilde, and Dylan, our part-time kitchen helper."

"Who came in while you were away?"

"Matilde."

"Where is she?"

"At her home, I imagine. She is due here at 4:00 pm."

"And Dylan?"

"I have no idea. He quit two days ago."

"Why?"

"He said he found a full-time job."

"Could I have the addresses for both of them? And don't mention to Matilde that I was here. I'm going to get someone up here to dust for prints. Should hers be up here?"

"No, I don't think so. Unless Andre sent her for something, but I can't think what."

"We'll ask her. What about Dylan?"

"He never left the kitchen."

Adam arranged for someone to come and go over the area where the boxes or crates had been. Meanwhile, he drove to the small apartment building where Matilde lived. Alone, Mary thought.

Matilde's neighborhood of late nineteenth-century homes looked to be in the first stages of gentrification. Most of the houses were compact bungalows with a few square feet of grass in front, some surrounded by newly-painted, wrought iron fences, some given over to tall weeds and crabgrass.

She lived in one of the few two-story homes, once grand, now converted to many apartments. A broken flagstone walk led past the unkempt lawn to a short flight of steps. The doorbell had been painted over so many times the button wouldn't budge.

A slight movement of the curtains of the first-floor apartment was the only sign of life in the building. Adam knocked, waited, and then knocked again. Nothing. As he turned to go down the steps, a querulous elderly voice called to him from the front window.

"What do you want?"

"Davidson, Culver's Mills police. Have you seen Matilde Gagnon today?"

"What's she done?"

"Nothing. I have a few questions for her?"

The door flew open, and a tiny elderly woman confronted him.

"No need to shout, young man."

"Sorry, ma'am. Have you seen her today, Mrs?"

"Armitage, Madge Armitage. No, and I don't care if I ever set eyes on that nosy, unfriendly woman again,"

"Nosy and unfriendly at the same time?"

"Oh, yes. Always asking if anyone had been around, knocking at her door or snooping around the place. Who would snoop around this place? And not even so much as a hello if you passed her on the street."

"Had anyone been around?"

"Not that I saw."

"Thank you for your help, Mrs. Armitage," Adam said, giving her his card. "Please call me if you think of anything else."

On his way back to the station, Adam considered Dylan Halpearn. He had been surprised to find him working in the kitchen of Evan's or, in fact, anywhere. He was about twenty, Adam thought, and in trouble off and on for the last ten years. His record as a juvenile would be sealed but Pete, whose memory was lengthy, would be able to tell him about every time he had found Dylan when he had answered a call. Not that Dylan was likely to be involved in a sophisticated art theft, not as the principal anyway. He parked beside Pete's Ford 150.

Anne and Brad huddled over a computer printout at one desk, while Pete, his face furrowed with concentration, punched keys at another. Office work wasn't his favorite part of the job.

"Anything on Matilde, Pete?"

"Nothing. I can't find her in the system anywhere. Do you have an employment record from the restaurant? I'm going to need her Social Security number."

"Yeah, I brought it," he said. "What do you know about a kid called Dylan Halpearn?"

"Too much. Kid lives out on Maple Road, near the Bassett place, with his grandmother. Always in trouble. Mostly minor stuff. He started drinking heavily when he was about fifteen after his mother died in a car accident. After that, I took him in a few times for drunk and disorderly, bar fights, underage drinking. Last time the judge met with the grandma and him and arranged for him to go to an alternative school. That's when he started in the cooking. Went to AA. Either that or jail. No trouble since then."

"He quit two days ago."

"Better go find him. I kinda liked the kid. Hoped he would stay straight."

"Maybe he has. He told Mary he got a better job."

Pete grimaced and shook his head.

"Sure he did."

* * *

Dylan's grandmother had a small but tidy property on the road to Bassett's but on the opposite side. A few chickens roamed a fenced-off part of the yard, guarded by a bone-thin mongrel dog. The hair on the back of the dog's neck rose as he circled the truck. Pete leaned on the horn.

The kitchen door opened and a tall, gaunt, woman, her grey hair hanging in loose braids down her back, came out and stood on the tiny porch, her arms folded tightly against her body.

"Oh, no. He's not in trouble again, is he, Sergeant Graham?"

"Not that I know, Mrs. O'Neill. I need to ask him some questions about the restaurant."

"He don't work there anymore."

"Where is he?"

"He went to Burlington to work in that big resort down there. One of the teachers from the school he was at when he went away, is running the kitchen there now and he called him to come and work for him. He's a good boy now."

"He was trying hard. Do you have an address for him?"

"I have a phone number."

"Can I have it, please?"

"All right," she said as she handed him the number. "So long as you aren't after him to charge him with something."

"Just a question."

When he called to the station, Adam told Pete to go to Burlington the next morning and check on Dylan. Adam wanted someone the boy knew to talk to him.

Chapter Twenty-Eight

The winding drive in from the four-lane took Pete through a copse of trees, under-planted with green plants and shrubbery, and past a few holes of a well-kept golf course. The sprawling red-brick inn, including the main house and two wings twice the length of the original building, overlooked Lake Champlain. His goal was the kitchen, but if there was a back entrance with trash cans and dumpsters, he couldn't see it.

He asked for directions from a crew working on the garden beds near the hotel entrance. A gardener pointed to a fieldstone arch, covered with red-leaved vines, opening into a cobblestoned square. Ahead, a discreet sign pointed to Executive Offices, Dining Rooms.

Pete hadn't noticed the driver of a black half-ton, waiting and watching from behind its darkened windows.

A blond woman, dressed in pink and grey to match the decor, sat behind an antique desk. Her nails clicked on the computer keyboard in the thick-carpeted silence.

"Ma'am," he said, using the softest voice he could.

"I'll be a moment."

"Graham, Culver's Mills Police,"

Pete interposed his identification between her and her monitor.

"Police? We didn't call the police."

"No, you didn't. I would like to speak to Mr. Porter, please."

"Oh, he's over in the kitchen at this time of the day."

The question answered she resumed her furious typing. A tiny frown spoiled her perfect forehead when Pete asked where the kitchens were.

"The quickest way is across the courtyard, past the dumpster and through the back door. He's busy, making the preparations for dinner. Is that all?

"Yes, thank you."

Pete walked through the kitchen door and into a wall of noise and white-hatted bodies, all working at incredible speed.

"Can you tell me where Mr. Porter is, please," he asked the closest, standing well back from the flying knife that was chopping garlic at a furious pace.

"Down there."

The knife pointed to the end of the kitchen and resumed its task.

No one paused in his work long enough to glance at the unexpected visitor. Pete headed for the end of the long room. The man-in-charge issued staccato orders as he moved from station to station.

"Mr. Porter?"

"Who are you?"

Pete introduced himself again and asked to speak to the chef privately.

"My office."

A desk and two chairs suggested it was an office, but white coats, kitchen equipment, and a wall of cookbooks took up most of the space.

"What's this about?" the chef said.

"I want to talk to you about Dylan Halpearn. He's here working for you?"

"Yeah, but if we're going to talk about him, I want him in here."

"Has he been here for the last four days?"

"Yeah, I called him to come down, and he was only too happy to leave that job. Someone was giving him a hard time."

"Do you know who?"

"Nah."

"Where does Dylan live?"

"He lives here, in the staff quarters for now. He has been on sixteen and off eight since he came."

"Long hours."

"It's a busy season for us, what with tourists coming to look at the leaves and all."

"Can you call him in here?"

The tall, well-nourished young man, dressed in whites and a chef's hat, bore little resemblance to the slouching, skinny kid Pete used to arrest for liquor offences.

"Hi," he said, putting out his hand.

"Dylan, good to see you," Pete said shaking his hand. "I wanted to ask you a few questions about Evan's."

"I was glad to see the last of that place. I had it with that old bitch."

"Mary?"

"No, Matilde. She thought she owned the place."

"Did you ever go up to the attics there?"

"Hell, no. Matilde had a fit if I left the kitchen to take a leak. The day I saw her take the box away, she lost it."

"What box? How big?"

"Three feet by four, five or six inches wide, maybe. She said it was hers when I asked what she was doing, and threatened she would tell Andre I wasn't clean in the kitchen if I said anything about her storing it in the attic. I guess Andre didn't know."

Pete's cell phone started to vibrate on his hip.

"Have you found Dylan?" Adam's voice on the phone.

"Yeah, he's with me here, and he's been here for four days, nonstop. He says Matilde took a crate out of the attic at Andre's."

"Then I think he's in some danger. Can you stash him somewhere safe and come back here as quick as you can?

"Will do."

Pete told Dylan and his boss about the need for some protection.

"I can let him stay in my apartment here. I rarely use it. It goes with the job," said Porter.

"Where is it?"

"Across the yard."

The three men had walked out from behind the screen when a worker called to Porter. As they turned back, a shot hit the wall where Dylan's head had been moments before, and the sound of a rifle filled the quiet courtyard.

"In, in. Get some police here," Pete shouted at the nearest white jacket. He turned and saw a black truck swerve and screech tires on its way back out the drive.

"Take him inside."

Pete ran for his truck, only to pound the side in frustration at his deflated front tire. He phoned a description of the truck to the police from the chef's office and went back to the shaking Dylan.

"Take it easy, Dylan."

"Take it easy. Somebody tried to kill me. What the hell for?"

"Because you saw Matilde take the crate out of Evan's. He may try again, but he's gone now. I'll ask the local police for protection."

Hours later, Pete drove back to Culver's, frustrated by the lack of progress in finding the shooter.

Chapter Twenty-Nine

The receptionist buzzed Adam to tell him Ted Atkins was at the desk and wanted to talk to him.

"Come in, Ted."

Ted had changed, Adam noticed. He had been a mess, drinking heavily, his depression mirrored in his sad face. He used to look as if he showered some time last week and visited a barber sometime last year. This was a new, spruced-up version. He even had a smile on his long face. Maybe a woman in his life?

"What can I do for you?"

"I wanted to tell you I'm writing a story about the boys who were missing."

Adam leaned over Ted, his face a dangerous shade of red.

"Those boys are still in danger. What do you think you are doing?"

"Take it easy, Adam. I'm not going to disclose where they're staying. I thought you would react like that, so I brought the copy. There's nothing identifying in it."

Adam took the papers from Ted and read quickly.

"Okay, so there is nothing that could identify the boys. Did Anne give you an interview?

Anne's head came up as she heard her name.

"Nothing much. Generic information about posttraumatic stress syndrome. Are the boys stashed with the aunt?"

"No comment, Ted. Your story is good as it stands. I have to get back to work."

"Okay."

Adam watched Ted's rapid progress across the office with amazement. He wondered who she was.

"I didn't tell him anything," Anne said.

"I know. What have you got so far today?"

"The Leclerc family tree has quite a few dead branches—family lines that petered out. I was able to construct a partial family tree from Mr. Trevelyan's information and the online census data. He isn't the sole heir."

"No?"

Anne showed him a family tree that included a small child, Alice, daughter of Mildred Hall and Aaron Bentley. She was still alive in 1900, but Anne couldn't find her in 1910.

"What now?"

"I want to find Alice. Lots of kids died young, or perhaps she married, so it's back to the church."

Brad took Anne to the Catholic Church, where she found, to her delight, the years she needed on computer disk. Alice married William Blakely in 1908, and that was the end of the trail. No baptisms followed, so no children, at least not in this parish.

On their way back to the office, she planned the next step in the search. A museum in New Hampshire had sent the sampler, so perhaps she would find traces in the census there.

The census, for 1910 in New Hampshire, was available through her Ancestry.com subscription and in the small town of Laconia, Belknap County, New Hampshire, she found them. The trail in the census was helpful, but newspaper records would fill in the gaps between the ten years from one census to another. Perhaps a trip to

New Hampshire, Anne thought as Brad drove her back to Catherine's.

Catherine's other guest, a visiting minister who filled in at one of the local churches, was checking out when Anne walked into the spacious front hall. Anne nodded and walked to the kitchen to make a phone call.

"Thank you, I'll see you in about half-an-hour."

Anne put the portable phone back in its cradle. Her face creased into a delighted smile as she turned to Catherine.

"I guess you and Thomas are talking again?"

"Yes, and he's going to fly me to New Hampshire."

"Save you the drive."

Anne decided the only way to further her knowledge of the Windeman genealogy was to drive to Laconia, Belknap County, New Hampshire and read the newspaper archives. She intended to leave after breakfast, but the early morning call from Thomas and his quick offer to fly her changed her plans.

Thomas picked her up in his favorite car, a silver Honda Prelude from the early nineties, lovingly restored.

"What's our mission today," he said.

"Intell."

"We'll be in time for an early lunch."

Thomas's plane was waiting on the tarmac when they arrived at the small municipal airport that served Culver's Mills. Anne had flown once before in Thomas's little red two-seater. She loved small planes and the feeling they gave her of being in the air, not a metal tube. Once they were up, she asked Thomas about their flight plan.

"Will we be flying over mountains today?"

"The Taconics are south of our route, the Green Mountains ahead. To the north are the Cold Hollow Mountains. When we get closer to New Hampshire, if the weather holds, we'll be able to see Mount Washington, in the White Mountains. It's the highest mountain in New England and home to some of the worst flying weather, so I'm going to stay to the south and take a little longer than usual."

Below them, the fertile farmland of the Champlain River Valley rose to the rolling foothills of the Green Mountains and then the mist-covered peaks of the mountains themselves.

"I'm sorry about what happened at the hospital."

"So am I. You were concerned about my injury, and I responded as if you tried to take over my life."

She turned to him and touched his arm.

"I have issues with control. It was a problem in my marriage and my relationship with the children. I want you to know I've had therapy and I haven't erupted like that for many years."

"I'm not used to that in a man in my personal life. Michael would have found it strange if I couldn't handle whatever came my way."

"So would I. It won't happen again."

"I won't let you bully me, Thomas, and I won't be around if it is a problem. Deal?"

"Deal."

"What's that river."

She pointed to a winding silver line.

"Connecticut. We're over New Hampshire now. If you look north, you can see Mount Washington."

"You said it had bad weather. It looks lovely."

"The weather at the summit includes gale to hurricane force winds, rain, snow—even in September—sudden changes in visibility. A little plane like this couldn't withstand what goes on up there."

"Your flight plan takes us to the south?"

"Yes, over the lower elevations of the mountains. We're almost there. Laconia is up ahead."

To the north and east, lay a broad expanse of water—Lake Winnipesaukee, Thomas said—and a small town near its shores. Other lakes and streams dotted the area, giving it the tourist name of the Lakes.

After they landed, Thomas picked up the car he'd arranged.

"Where to now?" he asked.

"The Gale Memorial building. It houses the library. I called ahead and arranged to look at their newspaper archive for the period I that interests me."

"It's on Main St. I found it described as a "fine example of the Romanesque Revival Style, using Deer Island granite, New Brunswick granite, oak paneling and stained glass windows." Red brick with rock facings and heavy arches. It also has a romantic tower. The man who built it must have had an interesting father. He gave him the name 'Napoleon Bonaparte Gale'. The building was constructed in 1903 and reminds me of the Post Office in Arnprior, Ontario, built about the same time, also with New Brunswick granite."

They covered the three miles to the city center, crossing a bridge and admiring the old mill and town hall reflected in the Merrimack River. Thomas drove off to explore the town and area while she climbed the steps to the main floor of the library. Directed to the archives, she was delighted to find the newspapers she ordered waiting for her, spread out on an oak table under tall, stained-glass windows. Almost like being in a church she thought.

Her first objective was to find the Blakelys, Alice and William. She thought a birth notice would be the most likely, starting a few months after the wedding date. The ill-fitting white gloves the library provided made her fumble-fingered and awkward as she turned the pages of the Laconia Democrat to scan the birth announcements in each issue. She found baby Arlene in 1910. Now for death or marriage.

By lunch-time, Anne had found the wedding of Arlene and David Windeman, in 1929. The notice said the bride and groom would reside with the bride's family. The librarian had a copy of the census of 1930, and Anne found them with infant daughter Marilyn.

After Thomas returned for her and took her to lunch at a delightful restaurant overlooking Lake Winnipesaukee, she searched for a wedding for Marilyn. She found her in 1949, married to Kurt Andrews, a soldier stationed nearby. Korea, Anne thought and searched forward through the war years. Sometimes a local paper would do a homecoming story.

Not this time. Kurt died in Korea in 1952. The story mentioned Marilyn but no children. She wondered what had become of her. The library had a collection of old phone books, but after the 1952 entry, there were no further Andrews listed.

Anne took the information, called Thomas and met him for a brief tour of the area before they flew back to Culver's Mills.

"Do you want to say over?" he asked.

They stopped to admire the classic white facade of the 1875 Inn at Tilton, the centerpiece of a small village near Laconia.

"No, I'm still tired by the end of the day and today has been full. Wouldn't it be lovely to come back here, though?"

"We'll put it on the list," he said as he turned the car around and headed for the airport.

"Is it more difficult to fly in the evening? That's when the Kennedy boy got into trouble, wasn't it?"

"Yes, it is, but I have instruments and many flying hours. Don't worry."

Chapter Thirty

Moments later they were flying, again south of the mountains, and west into a glorious red-gold and violet sunset. Anne had drifted off to sleep when a heart-stopping drop jolted her awake, and she clutched at Thomas.

"Sorry, dear heart, but we've run into a bit of unannounced weather."

Flashes of lightning illuminated mountains of black clouds and brief glimpses of fields and forests, swinging in and out of sight as the plane fought against the winds. Thomas shouted to her above the noise of the engine and the wind.

"I'll put down if I can. Watch on your side for anything that looks like a landing strip. We should be near an abandoned airfield at St. Johnsbury."

"Near a town?"

"Yes."

"No lights. Are we more or less on course?"

"I'm not sure. What with the wind and the lightning, we may be a little off. No mountains?"

"Not over here." Anne peered at the ground as the lightning flared.

"There's a long field to the right."

"Which way does it run?"

"From my right to your left."

The plane swung in a dizzying arc, and he shouted, "I see it. I'll put down if I can."

The radio crackled with static as he tried to Mayday. No response.

"Hang on."

The plane careered wildly in the crosswinds, then hit the ground, wing down on the left, but upright.

"Thomas?" Anne whispered, reaching for him in the darkness.

"I'm okay except for my head. You?"

"Okay."

"We have to get out. Smell the gas?"

He tugged at Anne's seat belt and released her.

"No."

Anne grabbed her backpack and followed him out and over the wing. Thomas lifted her off the wing and away from the plane.

"Run."

Then, she smelled it too and heard the faint crackle of flames somewhere behind them. The field around them was rutted from the recent rains. If it had been an airfield, it had been a long time ago. They stumbled, and Anne fell heavily to her knees. Thomas reached for her and pulled her to his feet.

"Come on."

The flames behind were high enough now to light the scene ahead with a faint orange. An explosion of sound and then the winds from the blast knocked them to the ground. Thomas covered Anne as debris fell around them.

When the thuds and sizzle of burning debris had stopped, they sat up, still clutching each other and stared back at the burning mass of metal.

"Luck, pure dumb luck," said Thomas, holding Anne tighter.

"Give yourself some credit. We could still be in there. Did you send a Mayday before we went down?"

"I don't think so. The storm was interfering with the transmission. Also, I'm not sure where we are."

"St. Johnsbury, I think you said."

"There should have been lights from the town. I'm not sure how far off-course the wind took us."

"Do you know which way is west?"

"No. What do you have that we can use? I haven't anything except a small knife and my wallet."

Anne inventoried her backpack: one cell-phone (out of range), one computer (no wireless ditto) a small flashlight, two granola bars and a bottle of water (half empty) and a Swiss army knife.

"This thing has a compass, I think."

She handed the knife to him.

"Yes. Northwest is that way."

He pointed to a path along the edge of the pasture. The faint glow from the burning plane faded out as the flames died under the onslaught of heavy rain. Lightning lit the fields, and then thunder roared and echoed around them.

"Thomas, we have to stay right here until this storm is over. We're far enough from the trees, and if we stay down, we won't be a target for the lightning."

Anne wiggled out of her soaking trench coat and spread it over them as they huddled together. What seemed like hours later, the rain abated, and the lightning moved off to the east.

"Let's move," Thomas said. "I think it's over."

"Yes. I'm freezing,"

Anne's teeth chattered as she took Thomas's hand and levered herself out of the mud.

The wind pushed the clouds away, and light from the emerging moon began to reveal the path ahead. Cows or something had made a trail along the side of the pasture. Anne hoped they were following it to the farmhouse, not away. When she said so, Thomas told her not to be too hopeful that the path had been made by barn-seeking cows.

"There are walking trails all over Vermont, and we could be on this one for miles before we came to a farmhouse."

"I'm hoping for cows."

All this for a little information on people long dead, Anne thought. Every time she got involved in these things she ended up in trouble. At least this time she hadn't gotten a concussion.

"How does your head feel?" she asked.

"Sore."

Anne aimed her light at him. Blood had oozed from a cut over his left eyebrow, mixed with mud from the field and caked on his face. He looked pale in the glare from the flashlight.

"If we find any water, I should wash some of that mud off you."

"Any left in the bottle? I'm getting thirsty."

The path they were following widened, and the walking became a little easier. When they paused again for a rest, Thomas said, "Listen, do you hear something?"

The wind had died, but no morning sounds of birds or animals filled the silence. What was he listening for? And then she heard it, the bubbling, rushing sound of water falling happily over stones.

"In here, I think."

He pushed aside some bushes, and Anne followed with the weak light from her failing flashlight. The path lay at the base of a long hill. Partway up, water dribbled down a rock face, gathered in a depression, and, over-full, splashed in a miniature waterfall before it gathered itself to form a stream. Thomas scrambled up to the little basin, cupped his hands and drank.

"Throw me the bottle," he called, turning to find Anne at his elbow.

"Let me get a little of that blood and muck off you."

She wiped his face and head with the tail of her shirt. "Not that there's much less mud on this shirt."

"I'm so sorry."

179

He held her tightly against him.

"Not your fault. I was thinking a while ago that every time I do some research in one of these cases I end up in an accident of some sort. It's my bad luck, not yours."

"I should have checked the weather again before we took off."

"You listened to it on the way to the airport. No reason to check it again. We're both alive, and except for your head and the blisters on my feet, we're okay. Let's go and see if we can find some civilization. I'd no idea that it was possible to be so far from anyone in Vermont. It looks so full of towns and villages when you fly over it at night."

Anne stopped babbling when Thomas kissed her.

"Now, let's go," he said and took her hand.

The sky to the east brightened to lavender, promising dawn. Their trail had taken them into and out of the woods, and across other fields, with no sign of a light to suggest another human being. They came to a stop sign indicating the end of the path at a paved road.

"I think we've been following a snowmobile trail."

"Which way."

"West."

"There is no west. It runs north and south."

"Then we'll go north. Burlington has to be north of our last position."

"North it is," said Anne as she shrugged into her pack.

Chapter Thirty-One

"Whoever this guy is, he doesn't care who he shoots at," Pete said to Adam as they went over the events at the hotel. "He followed me, and he shot at Dylan with me standing right there. Some bodyguard I am."

"Don't be so hard on yourself. What if he wasn't following you and found Dylan on his own? Did you find out if anyone had been asking about him at his grandma's or the hotel?"

"I asked at the hotel, but not his grandmother. She didn't volunteer it. I'll go out and see her, tell her Dylan is safe and not to talk to anyone."

"Okay. Brad, what do you have on today?"

"Court. I've got a pair of fourteen-year-olds who stole the bingo cards, the teenage mother up on welfare fraud—that's a sad case—two traffic accidents over in the other court, and a DUI."

"Why did you lay a charge in the bingo card thing? Seems minor."

"Yeah, I warned both of them before. One of them needs to go to residential, and the mom put it off for years. I figure it's his last chance. The other one is headed for the life. He's mentally slow, and his dad's a drug dealer."

"You'll be all day if you can get from court to court. I'm still working on Matilde and the connection between the break-in at Evan's and the theft of the pictures."

The briefing over, Adam looked through reports from the National Crime Information Center on the individuals in the case. He had sent for anything they had on Andre, Mary, Matilde and Janice. Nothing on Andre as an adult. Mary and the other two women weren't in the NCIC system.

Matilde and Janice weren't in any system, except for driver's license. Janice got a replacement when she moved to Vermont three years ago.

Routine filled most of the day, and it was about eight o'clock when Adam took a call from Catherine.

"Adam, I'm so glad I caught you. Have you seen Anne after her trip to New Hampshire?"

"No, did you expect her back by now?"

"Yes, she thought they would be back in time for dinner but there's been quite a storm to the east, and I'm a little worried."

"Perhaps they decided to stay over and haven't called you yet."

"That's not like Anne."

"Maybe they're having dinner. Call me back if you don't hear from her by nine."

Adam gave her his cell number to call. As he said good-night to the desk clerk who was coming on for the evening shift, the phone rang again on his line.

"Do you want to take this, Lieutenant? Mrs. Beauchamp."

"Yes."

"Lieutenant, I'm worried about Anne and my son. They're overdue on their trip back from New Hampshire."

Again, Adam tried to calm the fear, mentioning dinner, the romantic little town, etc.

"No. Thomas left New Hampshire. I phoned the airport. He filed a flight plan and left several hours ago now. I expected him home at seven-thirty. He must be in New York on business tomorrow afternoon, and he hasn't cancelled the appointment."

"I'm on it, Mrs. Beauchamp, and I'll call you back when I learn something."

"Where will you start?"

"At the airport."

When he got off the phone, Adam told the desk clerk to call Brad and Pete back to the office. They both had long days. The defense called a medical witness in the bingo card case, and the doctor went on and on, reviewing what seemed to be every year in the life of the two boys. Brad hadn't made it to any other case.

Pete reported that the grandmother told a telephone caller where her grandson was.

The caller was a man, she said. He didn't give a name but said he was a friend of Dylan's.

"What's up, boss?" Brad said when he came through the door, steps ahead of Pete.

"Anne and Thomas are missing. They left New Hampshire, but never arrived here. I called search and rescue, and I'm going out to the airport to work with them. Brad, you work the computer, looking for places they could put down between here and New Hampshire. Pete, call all the airfields, large and small between here and there."

The two men started their jobs in grim silence. Adam watched them for a moment then left, calling Catherine on his cell as he went.

"I'm coming to the airport," she said.

"I'll call you."

"No, I'm coming."

In Vermont, all missing persons were reported to State Police whose search and rescue units work with other agencies such as the Upper Valley Wilderness Response Team.

Adam called the State Police, who were setting up their mobile command post at the airport, preparing to move once they had a general idea of where the missing persons were. Some of their people were doing the same jobs he gave to Brad and Pete, but Brad was gifted on the computer and Pete tenacious as a pit bull at getting the information he needed.

Adam found Lieutenant Jacqueline Dupuis, team leader, in charge. He'd worked with her before.

"Anything you've learned that could help us narrow this search?" she said, shaking his hand.

"No. The man's mother said he filed a flight plan and left the airport in Belknap County. I think you already have that?"

"Yes. Could you help us with the press and the families?"

"Sure. Anne has a sister in Bermuda. Her husband is dead, and she has no children. There may be some other relatives. Her friend will be out here soon, and I think she'll know if we should call anyone. Thomas's family knows. How does it look?"

"If they went down uncontrolled in the storm, they didn't survive," she said.

"He's a good pilot."

"Then let's hope he was able to set her down."

The storm was passing, and the helicopter was airborne when Catherine arrived. He shook his head at her when she reached him.

"Nothing yet, Catherine. I'm so sorry. They want to know if there is any family we should call."

"Her cousin in Toronto. I told him I would call if we had any news."

"What about her sister?"

"Time enough, later."

They sat on two of the hard plastic chairs in the waiting area, staring out at the darkening sky.

"What the hell, Adam? What have you got her into this time?"

Ted banged open the outer door.

"Take it easy. I didn't send her to New Hampshire. She wanted some information and went for a day's outing with Thomas Beauchamp. And she loves to fly."

"Sorry, I sort of feel responsible for her after last year. What's the story?"

Adam gave him what he had, which was little, and the reporter went to call it in.

Catherine was a pacer: back and forth in front of the long windows, peering out at the runways, empty of planes and dimly lit, over to the board the search and rescue team was keeping of sightings and follow-ups, and back again. Adam interrupted her steady march.

"Catherine, would you like something to eat?"

"No, thank you, I couldn't. Why haven't they found the plane? This isn't Alaska for heaven's sake."

"The storm."

His phone rang.

"Adam? Brad. Pete's called all the airfields, even the ones that close at night. Nothing. There are some abandoned fields. One looks good, at St. Johnsbury, but I can't raise anyone. Could you get a trooper to go and look?"

"Sure."

Adam walked over to the small office where Jacqueline was working. Her trim, controlled figure hunched over her computer as she talked on her phone. One of her staff stood waiting, his report a dismal two lines.

"What's up," she asked.

"One of my guys says there's a field at St. Johnsbury. Can you call the state police to check it out?"

"That's right on their flight path. They couldn't land there in the storm, but sure, we'll check."

Brad didn't say anything about his work, but Adam knew he was at his computer, finding surveillance pictures, looking for fields big enough for the small plane to land.

He wasn't surprised at another call.

"Boss, it's me again. Pete got a call from one of his buddies in the state police. They got a report of a possible plane crash and a fire north of St. Johnsbury. Noone's been out there yet."

Brad's voice choked as he finished his report.

"I'll tell Search."

He walked over and told the information to Jacqueline.

Catherine waited by the window. As he walked towards her, he saw her cross herself. Maybe prayer was all they had.

"The state police reported a possible plane crash north of St. Johnsbury," he told her, "but nothing definite."

"Should we call Mrs. Beauchamp?"

"I don't think so. Let's wait until the state police call."

More hours passed, more waiting. Police reported a fire in a farmer's field, called in by the owner when he found his cows inspecting the remains of the plane. No bodies. Adam called Mrs. Beauchamp.

"Adam, can we drive up there? I would like to be close by if they find Anne," said Catherine.

"Sure."

Anything was better than this, he thought. Before he left, he called Brad.

"Catherine and I are going to drive out to the crash. Keep in touch."

Three hours later, they stopped in front of the police barracks on route 5. The trooper at the desk directed them to the site, north-west of St. Johnsbury, called Caledonia, and as lonely as its British namesake. A scattered thirty thousand people shared the still rural landscape. Catherine stared through the car windows at the wreckage, appalled at the twisted mass of flame-marked steel. How had they ever escaped, she thought? No bodies, the trooper said. Adam was talking to the police officers and conferring with the searchers who emerged from the bush that lined the short field.

The trooper showed Adam the path along the side of the pasture. Under a bit of shelter from dense overhanging trees, he found traces of footprints, not enough to identify, but enough to show walkers had passed through, likely since the storm let up. It was a snowmobile path, he said, but walkers shared it with ATVs in the summer.

"Where does it lead."

"It ends at Route 15."

"Could they walk that far, overnight?"

"If neither of them was injured. If they turn north, there's no town and few homes until they reach Nevesville, and even that is off the highway. We sent a car along there early this morning, but we didn't see anyone."

"Maybe they hadn't reached the road yet. Are you sending an ATV along the trail?"

"Yes, sir. It'll be along."

Adam walked back to where Catherine waited for him, her anxious face peering at him through fogged windows.

Adam told her what he learned from the police and said they would drive Route 15 again.

It was 10:00 am by the time they reached the junction of the trail with Route 15.

"Which way, Adam?"

"I think they would have walked north, assuming home lay that way. The troopers searched to the south because they knew a town lay a few miles in that direction. Anne and Thomas may not have realized that," he said as he accelerated north.

Chapter Thirty-Two

Anne and Thomas trudged in silence along the side of the highway through a bone-chilling early morning mist.

"I think we are the only living creatures in this part of the state," Anne said "Not even a highway patrol or a logging truck."

"They'll be looking for us. Maybe we should have stayed with the plane."

"They can find us on this road, then. I couldn't sit there in the mud all night long. No one saw us go down in the storm, or the fire either. The rain put it out too soon."

"I'm saying it might have been smarter."

"And I'm saying we were too cold, too wet and too thirsty to stay there. This is a road. Surely the state didn't build a road to nowhere."

"Hey, we decided to walk, not you."

"We didn't decide; we got up and left. I don't remember deciding. There was no deciding going on."

Her body shook and tears coursed down her face.

"I don't know why I am crying, except I'm tired and hungry and scared for no reason. And mad as hell."

Thomas held her, saying, "I'm tired and hungry and angry, too. Let's try to be angry at the road or the weather or the State of Vermont, instead of each other."

"We could write a letter to the Governor."

And so they did, walking along the roadside, shouting angry phrases, shaking their fists, and dissolving into laughter as they blamed the governor for the storm, the crash, the mud and the road to nowhere.

Anne tried her cell phone again and threw it back in her pack in disgust. Still no service. It was mid-morning, and they'd met no traffic.

"I think this road ends somewhere out here and there is no town."

"I'm beginning to remember this road now. My dad used to do business in St. Johnsbury, and I would go with him now and then. This was when I was maybe ten years old. We stopped in a town called Nevesville for ice-cream. After that, there was a long boring stretch. This is the same road. Or looks a lot like it."

"Ice-cream sounds nice. And look at those lovely rocks up ahead, begging for someone to sit on them."

"Want to set awhile, ma'am?

"I surely do," she said as she replied in her best mock-Southern accent.

And that is how Adam and Catherine found them, sitting on a flat rock in the sun, their backs against the boulder behind them, holding hands and talking.

Yet another visit to a Vermont hospital, Anne thought. Soon the insurance company would think she was too big a risk for international travel. Thomas was sitting in his curtained space, enduring the suturing of his head laceration.

She insisted she was unhurt, but a seat belt bruise across her abdomen triggered an ultrasound. A gentle nurse cleaned the blood off her feet where blisters formed and burst and bled during their long walk. The doctor came and went, assuring her the ultrasound was normal and she could go as soon as Thomas 's suturing was done. His CAT scan was normal.

A knock came at the door to the room. Adam and Catherine poked their heads through the gap in the curtains.

"You two look like children at a Christmas concert," Anne said. "Come in. Thomas will be finished in a few minutes, and we can go home."

"How are you feeling?"

"Fine but in desperate need of some Tim's. The nurse warned me against the hospital's coffee."

"Did you phone my mother?" Thomas said. "I don't think she believed me when I told her I was fine."

"Yes," Adam said as he stepped around the curtain. "I think she's convinced. I persuaded her to wait until I delivered you to her front door."

"Thanks. She's been against my flying since I took it up. I'm never going to hear the end of this."

Thomas shook his head at the thought of his mother's response to the crash.

"Hold still," the doctor said.

Half an hour and some bill-paying later, they were on their way back to Culver's Mills. Anne fell asleep and woke up as Adam parked in the driveway at Catherine's.

"Time to go to bed," Adam said, taking Anne's backpack from the trunk.

"I have so much information to go through."

"Tomorrow."

Chapter Thirty-Three

Every bone ached, and muscles Anne hadn't remembered for years protested her every move as she sat up in response to the quiet rap at her door. Catherine drifted in like a benevolent ghost, bringing breakfast and opening her curtains to a bright pink morning. She deposited the tray on the white wicker table beside Anne's bed.

"You said you wanted me to call you by ten, but I still don't know what's the rush."

"I have some information I want to go over."

"It can't wait?"

"I'm sure it can but I can't. I've had it, Catherine. I want to go home, and I want to finish what I started here. If this ageing body will move for me. I hope I didn't carry that pack all those miles for nothing."

"Are you working here this morning? I'm due at the shelter."

"No, I'll go down to the station. Brad will help me with some of it."

* * *

Anne drove over to the courthouse and entered the squad room to a round of applause from the staff.

"Glad you made it," Pete said as he shook her hand.

"Thank you. You all worked hard to find us. I'll never forget it."

Through the rest of the day, she worked at Brad's computer, searching databases on Ancestry.com, for a trace of Marilyn Andrews. What would a woman do in 1952, widowed so young? Remarry. Anne found no record of a wedding in the Laconia paper.

"Brad, I'm looking for a Culver's Mills connection. Maybe Vermont relatives on her father's side?"

"Worth a shot."

A deputy escorted Anne across to the Library and waited, watching while she searched through phone books and city directories. In 1966 she found a phone number for Marilyn Andrews. Nothing in 1967. Did she stay in Culver's or did she remarry?

The newspaper archive was next. Anne turned the pages of the local paper for 1966. No mention anywhere, until she hit New Year's Day, 1967. She found a marriage notice for Marilyn Andrews, nee Windeman, and Peter Webb.

Webb. Nancy Webb was in the diner the day she reacted to the perfume. She was at the antique show too, talking to the librarian who died. What if she were another heir? What if she attacked her? Whoa. Going ahead of the data again, and imagining way too much on too little evidence.

Find the evidence. More patient page turning brought her to a birth announcement in October of the same year for a daughter, Nancy.

Anne met Adam at the courthouse steps and poured out her dates and connections.

"Stop. The last person found, the Trevelyan cousin, is Nancy Webb."

"Yes."

"Do you think she was listening to you?"

"I'm not sure she was listening. She was at the antique show, and at Lil's both times I reacted, but I can't say she was the one who wore the scent. It could have been aftershave or cologne. The librarian who died was there both times as well."

"She is a Leclerc descendent?"

"Oh, yes, unless there is a wild coincidence of names."

Adam raised an eyebrow.

"Possible."

"Yes, I suppose."

"Don't look so disappointed. We'll ask Nancy where her mother was born."

"If she knows."

Anne limped down the steps to where Thomas waited for her beside his car.

"Are you feeling rough? We can skip dinner if you don't feel up to it."

"Oh, no. I have trouble with my leg on stairs and the blisters of course, but otherwise, I'm fine. How are you?"

The bandage was off the row of neat stitches that closed his head wound.

"My head aches a bit but otherwise okay. What are your plans?"

As they drove the short distance to the Beauchamp home, Anne told him she planned to leave as soon as she finished the genealogy work and wrote a final report that tied up all the loose ends.

Twilight bathed the Beauchamp home in pink and amber, reflecting off the granite stones and mullioned windows, as they stopped in front of the bright blue door.

"Your home is so lovely, Thomas."

"It's always a pleasure to come home, just to look at it. Mother wondered if she should sell it and move to New York, but the kids and I encouraged her to stay here."

"It would be a shame if the house left the family. One of your ancestors built it, I assume?"

"Yes, my great-great-grandfather."

"I'm surprised he left it so your mother could sell it. Most men of his generation left property in the male line."

"I haven't thought about that. I've always called it Mother's house and was so young when Dad died I wasn't involved in the financial side. Let's leave it for now."

They walked down the hall to the living room where his mother waited.

* * *

Adam drove to the library, trying to remember what he knew about Nancy's family. Her mother died a few years before Adam's parents. They were older than most of the parents in his crowd. Her father died last year. He kept a small hardware store all the time Adam knew him.

Nancy worked for her father, summers and between semesters at college. She'd started her career somewhere, Burlington, he thought, before she came back to Culver's Mills. Never married, or he didn't think so. Hard to believe she would be involved in international art theft. Canada counted as international.

The library was closing as he walked through the old oak door. The lady at the desk stood up to head him off but sat down when she recognized him.

"Is Ms. Webb in?"

"Yes, she is. Shall I call her for you?"

"No thanks."

Adam walked to the door of the office, gave a short, hard rap and walked in.

Nancy's indignant voice assaulted him as she glared at him.

"What do you think you are doing, barging in here?"

He sat down in one of the oak armchairs across from her.

"I came to ask you where you were the day Jim Trevelyan and Anne McPhail were attacked."

"Where was I?"

Nancy's shocked and puzzled face surprised Adam. He suspected she might be involved because of the relationship with Trevelyan they discovered, but her surprise seemed genuine enough.

"Why should I tell you?" she said, steadying her voice. "I don't answer to you for my whereabouts."

Those nervous hands were at it again, this time playing with a short strand of amber-colored beads.

"Then would you tell me your mother's maiden name? No objection to that is there?"

"My mother? What on earth do you want with her name?"

"It's a simple question of identification. The sooner you answer; the sooner I'll be out of here."

"She was a widow when she married my father. Her name had been Windeman."

Nancy's eyes strayed to a wedding picture of a young couple in the clothes of the fifties that stood on a bookcase. Her parents, he presumed.

"Have you looked into your genealogy?"

"No. I am far too busy with the present, to ever be able to spend my time looking into the past."

Adam remembered she had been almost ousted from her job by an assistant librarian who was murdered last year. That woman had been a genius at genealogical research. Maybe Nancy didn't want to compete in that field too.

"Anne McPhail searched for descendants of the original owners of Evan's. You're one and have the same claim as James Trevelyan."

Color flooded her face as her shrill voice rose again.

"That's why you're asking me where I was. You think I would kill an old man for a house."

"Or whatever was hidden in the house."

"Hidden? I have no idea what you are talking about. I was in Burlington for two days, including the day they were attacked. I can give you a list of the people I was with."

She scribbled on a notepad, broke one pencil lead, and took another from a jar on her desk.

"Then I won't have to bother you anymore."

He reached across the desk for the paper then stood up to go.

"Can I talk to Anne McPhail about the genealogy?"

"You can ask. What she tells you is up to her."

* * *

Adam drove to Burlington after the interview with Nancy. He wanted to talk to Alisse before his law class. He found her in a private room in the Fletcher Allen Health Center, looking pale, but still elegant, in spite of the lack of make-up and the surgery to remove the bullet from her shoulder.

"Thank you for seeing me, Ms. Bertrand."

"What can I do for you, Lieutenant?"

Somehow she sounded more French today. Fatigue, he supposed.

"I wanted to ask you if your husband ever mentioned some people to you. Does the name Matilde Gagnon mean anything to you?"

"Matilde? I don't think so. There is a Matilde who is a server in the restaurant in Culver's Mills. Is that who you mean?"

"Yes."

"No, he never mentioned her, and I wouldn't have thought she was to his taste."

"I wasn't thinking of her as his lover, but as a conspirator."

She squeezed her eyebrows into a frown.

"Conspirator. But I told you I didn't know about his criminal activities."

"Yes, I know. Sometimes you know things but are unaware of the significance. What about a man called Bassett?"

"Bassett. Once a man called us at home, on our private line, and John was very angry with him. I think his name was Bassett."

"Do you know why your husband was so angry?"

"He told me that he didn't want people who were business associates to call us at home."

"He used that phrase, business associates?"

"The French equivalent, yes."

"What about Dan Abbott?"

"No."

"You thought your husband was having an affair. Did you have a name to go with that suspicion?"

"Once, late at night, I heard him talking on his cell-phone. From his tone, I knew it was a woman. I think he called her Janice or Jane, some name like that."

Her eyes filled with tears and she turned away from him.

"Could you go now? I'm exhausted."

"Sure. Thank you for your help," Adam said as he stood up.

His thanks went unanswered. Not too bad, he thought. Some confirmation of a link between Bassett and Andrews, and possibly between Janice Maynard and Andrews.

Adam left the hospital and made the short drive to the office of his academic adviser.

The law faculty of the University of Vermont was brand-new, and Adam was one of the first students to enrol in the part-time law degree. That had worked well in the first year, but now, at the end of the second, he felt that he wasn't going to get all he could from the degree if he didn't attend full time.

His advisor agreed and suggested that Adam consider a leave of absence from his job for the next year.

Chapter Thirty-Four

The woman's body rocked gently in the water, disturbed by a soft wind that had come up overnight. It drifted downstream towards the mill but paused in its journey at a curve, caught up on a submerged tree limb. The current tugged at it for an hour or more, and then sent it onwards towards the millpond. The wind pushed it onto a deadhead in the small bay where Anne had hidden, and there the body rested.

A dog lifted her nose from the fascinating scents along the walking path. Something new in the air today. Something that made her anxious. Whining, she tugged on the leash, eager to search the thickets on the bank of the pond.

"What's up with this dog?"

"Something's wrong," his wife said. "She sounds upset."

"Follow her in."

The retractable leash had allowed the dog to wander far ahead of them and now she started to bark.

"What now?" he said.

"You look, if you want. I'm not going in there."

A moment later, his wife returned, dragging the reluctant dog.

"There's a body in there. Call the police."

Matilde had gone into the water alive but unconscious, the ME thought. The head injury had been pre-mortem and she had drowned. Her lungs were full of river water. A shocked and silent crew listened to the ME's report.

Pictures of the dead and dying stared down at them from a corkboard. Anne sat at the rear.

When the medical examiner had left them, Captain Naismith summed up their case; two murders, two assaults and one dead in a car accident. The last would be investigated by the county, both because of the locale and because Adam had been involved.

"Did we get anything from the corpse in the car?"

"No," Brad replied. "The dental records confirmed that it was Abbott."

"What physical evidence do we have?"

"Fingerprints at scene one, plus two hairs. Nothing on Matilde. The river took care of that. Shell casings in the mill. Fingerprints at Trevelyan's that matched those at scene one."

He pointed in turn to pictures of the dead art dealer, Matilde, the mill and Trevelyan.

"What next?" Naismith asked Adam.

"We have a crew at Matilde's home. Pete's going over there. Brad will get some help and canvass the river bank upstream from where we found her. The ME thought she had been in the water about eight hours. There was a bit of wind last night. We figure that she came three miles max, less if she got hung up on anything.

I'm going over to her apartment with Pete. I think those paintings are the key to this, so we're going to be looking for them, or anything that links her to them. I figure she may have had a storage locker, so we'll be looking for a key."

"Keep me in the loop."

~

"Will do."

If Matilde had a criminal career, she hadn't spent the gains on her home, a cramped bachelor apartment in the old house with enough of everything for one—a sofa-bed, reading light, tiny table, television and one over-stuffed chair. Same in the cupboards—the sort of dishes you could buy in packages at the grocery store, with four of everything. Nothing on the walls, no computer. No clues at all into the woman's life or personality.

There were lots of clues to an intruder, though. Drawers were opened and the contents dumped, and the sofa slashed. The refrigerator stood open and the nauseating stench of decaying food and spoiled milk filled the room.

"We're looking for something like a locker key, that might connect her to a storage area," he told the crew.

Would she keep it in her apartment? If it were at Evan's, it would take days to find. If it existed. He went outside and started in again from the street, looking for a reasonable place to hide a small object where it wouldn't be found accidentally.

The house had been converted to apartments long ago. Three concrete steps, with an iron railing on one side, led up from the street to a flagstone walkway interrupted by weeds, grass and an occasional tiny remnant of ornamental planting between the stones. He tried the stones as he walked along, but none was loose.

Trash and a bicycle rack stood alongside unpainted steps up to a locked entrance. A rusting mailbox was tacked on the wall beside a doorbell that didn't work. Where would she hide a house-key, he wondered, as he searched behind the stairs and under the little porch.

The path continued as a dirt track beside the house and on past an old maple tree. A careless robin had built a nest on a low-hanging branch. Pale blue shells lay shattered on the ground.

He could easily reach the nest, but Matilde was shorter.

A step-stool leaned against the house. Possible. Deep in the feathers and fur lining the nest he found a small key, the kind that fits a padlock.

Pete called him. "Adam, the crew's done here. We didn't find anything like a key."

"Okay."

As he came around the side of the porch, he told Pete to stay behind so they could have one final look at the apartment.

"I got it. She hid it in a bird's nest," he told Pete when they were inside.

"Looks like a padlock key."

"Yeah. What about self-storage units?"

"The big outfits, like Hanes and Murphy's, have good dead bolt locks, but that small one out by the motel where we found Andrews might use something like this. It's for a cheap lock."

A row of bright-orange storage lockers—thin metal walls and a concrete pad, fronted with garage-style doors—stood behind a small equipment rental business. The owner identified the key as one of his. The number on the key corresponded to locker ten.

He opened a grubby file folder. The unit had been rented by Cerise Lebray one year ago. No, they didn't clock the renters in and out. The property was open 24/7.

"Not much security," Pete commented,

"Most people store old junk. You want security, you go to Hane's. Here's ten. Don't you guys have to have a search warrant or something?"

"Lebray's dead. We can take it from here," he said as the now-curious owner started to tag along as they walked across the unpaved lot towards the rows of lockers. Adam waited until the owner got it.

"Oh, yeah, okay. I'm outa here."

Number ten was the last in the first row. The door hadn't been opened for a few days. Dirt and leaves from the recent storm came up with it. Two crates stood against the back wall of the locker, the sole occupants of the eight-foot square space. They hadn't been there long. Very little dust had settled over the tops, although the floor had enough to show footprints.

"Call the crew," Adam instructed. "We're not going in until we can get shots of those footprints, and anything on the door and crates."

As Pete started out the door, a shot hit his chest, spinning him around and throwing him to the ground. Adam dragged him inside the locker and got the door down, as he shouted for help into his shoulder radio.

Adam yanked up Pete's shirt, wadding it around the wound, calling his name. Pete's skin was ashen, his breathing shallow and uneven. Where the hell was that ambulance?

"Come on, Pete," he urged. "Hang on, buddy."

A second shot hit the door. Another shot. What kind of madman thought killing cops would help in his situation? He could hear the sirens now. Moments later the door on the storage unit started up. Adam got to his feet, aiming his Glock at the door.

"Relax, Lieutenant, it's us," the paramedic voice assured him as his feet came into view.

The manager of the rent-all place stood beyond the police lines. Shaking and stumbling over his words, he tried to convince Adam that he had nothing to do with the shooting.

"A truck rolled up, Lieutenant. Next thing I knew, a guy in a black mask grabs a rifle and starts shooting. I went down behind the counter and stayed there until the ambulance came.

"Did he see you?"

"I don't think so."

"License plate."

"I got the first numbers. It was a Ford 150, black."

"What else did you see? What did he look like?"

"Thin, not tall. He had on a hat, not a baseball cap, one of those floppy hats that old guys wear. Heavy blue jacket and jeans. That's all I saw before I hit the floor."

"Okay. Anything else, you call."

"Okay."

Adam ran back to check Pete. The paramedics were finished hooking him up and inserting their lines. Moments later they were on their way. Adam walked to the back of the storage area and slit open the top of one of the crates. That one held the missing sampler. He left the other one for the crew to take in, and walked back to the office area. Brad met him at the door.

Brad got a bulletin out on the truck and used his in-car computer to find a list of possibles in the area. The one that stood out belonged to Janice Maynard.

What did a travel agent need with a truck? Anne noticed her near the mill after the shooting and worried that Maynard had overheard her conversation with Catherine.

"We'll check the Maynard woman first," he told Brad.

The shop was the only address that they had for her. An apartment above could be hers.

The parking lot behind the shop exited into a back lane. Brad parked the cruiser across the narrow entrance. The Ford stood by the back door.

"See if you can get anyone from the shooting to back us up here. She may be inside. Was there any other vehicle listed to her?"

"No."

Brad called for backup, but a lone cruiser, with Dave Graham at the wheel, was all the back-up that could be spared. Together they made a careful entry into the building. Steep stairs ended in a closed door. Brad kicked the door with his heavy boot while Adam squeezed tight behind him.

The place was empty. A featureless apartment, devoid of any personal items other than clothes and makeup, gave no leads to the woman who lived there. She took little with her as far as they could tell. An empty suitcase stood in a front closet; the dressers and closets were full of her flamboyant clothing. Adam left for the station, leaving Brad and Dave to finish.

Chapter Thirty-Five

Bassett couldn't stay long in his buddy's cabin. The cops would be all over that shore as soon as they found the boat. He spent summers here with his dad and knew every inch of the forest and the land to the north. He filled his pack with more supplies from the cabin, slung a rifle he found in the cache his friend kept hidden under the cabin and walked. Several miles further on was another lake and beyond that a third. All had cabins that wouldn't be used that time of year. He could break into one and lie low for a while or find a vehicle to steal.

By evening he reached the second lake. Far behind him, he heard dogs for a while, but a detour through a beaver meadow and up a stream took care of them. He needed a place to sleep. He started around the shore, trying to remember where the camps were on this lake.

He'd reached the remorseful stage, but his thoughts were still full of rage at his wife and the cops. His boys. Why did he take them? That was what he was sorry about. If he had left them at home, he could have gone back and taken them anytime. The social workers would get at them.

He stopped at the edge of a clearing. Smoke spiraled into the darkening sky from the chimney of the tiny cabin. A battered truck sat out the back. He watched for a while. No dog outside. A man left, walked to the outhouse and after a time, back again. No one Bassett knew. The sun dropped behind the trees; the light failed. Still, he waited, for that final trip to the outhouse, for the inside lights to go off, for quiet. A tiny red truck, battered and scraped, stood a little distance from the cabin. The light from his flashlight reflected off keys in the steering column. He eased up the door handle and gave the door an experimental tug. The teeth-grating screech of metal on metal brought outraged barking from the cabin.

The cabin light came on, and the door flew open.

"Who's out there? Get away from my truck."

Bassett turned, firing towards the voice.

"What the fuck? Take the damn truck."

The panicked voice was lost in the slam of the door, and the sudden darkness as the interior light went off again.

Bassett opened the door, cranked the key in the ignition, and drove off down the dirt track that served as a lane to the cabin. What seemed like a mile later, he hit a gravel road.

Now what? That guy had a phone or a radio. Cops would start looking for him up here. Now he'd have to change vehicles again.

A few miles more, he stopped worrying about them linking him with the theft of the truck. Why would they, he thought? Just another kid stealing a truck, forgetting the shot he took at the owner. He needed a place to stay. He'd make sure there was no one home at the next cabin.

He was a hundred miles from Culver's Mills when he took the Round Lake Rd. He knew that one well, too. No permanent homes at all, the last time he was up here. Three or four rough cabins, no water, no electricity. The shoreline was a swamp, with the ducks and the bugs the usual occupants. He knew that if he drove further, maybe ten miles, there was a crossroads, a gas station and a little general store. He could risk getting some supplies when he ran out. People up here were inclined to mind their own business.

What was he going to do? What happened to the boys? He didn't want to go to Canada without them, but it would make it harder to cross the border if they traveled with him.

He had reached that point in his thinking when he spotted a dirt track off to the left. Likely a trail into a camp. He made the turn and ended at a small clearing. No smoke from the chimney and no one came out to investigate the strange truck in the yard. He waited a little longer, and then, cradling the rifle in one arm, he walked up to the door. Unlocked. A sign inside read:

Help yourself but leave it the way you found it.

That wouldn't be a problem. It looked like his: a few basic pieces of furniture, mismatched plates and so on, mattresses on bunk beds in the next room, outhouse. Cans of food in the cupboard and an old wood stove in the corner with a small stack of firewood beside it meant he wouldn't be cold or hungry for a while. He looked for a well and found a pump behind the house. Perfect. He threw himself on one of the sweat-soaked mattresses. After a time, he slept.

Adam took a call from Prescott Jones, the sheriff in the county to the north.

"Adam, we lost the bugger. He took to the swamps, and the creeks and the dogs lost the scent."

"Yeah, my guys tell me he's quite a hunter and knows all that country up there."

"He has to surface sometime. We'll keep looking."

"Let me know."

The old man behind the counter looked up as the screen door slammed. A burly, bearded man in a dirty plaid work- shirt and faded jeans walked up to the counter as he had every morning for several days now, bought one pack of cigarettes, a newspaper and a coffee, and went outside to sit on a bench in the sunshine. He hadn't answered the question about who he was, and no one knew where he lived. The store was the only one around for thirty miles, and the few customers were hunters and fishermen on their way in or out to their camps. This guy didn't seem to be on his way to anywhere.

A sudden burst of profanity startled the shopkeeper. Bassett raged outside the door, tearing the newspaper into shreds and shaking his fist. The shopkeeper reached for the shotgun he kept under the counter, but Bassett ran across to his truck and roared off down the dirt road.

"Wonder what set him off?" the old guy said as he looked through his copy of the paper. The front page held Ted Atkins' story about the missing boys and their father. The description fit that guy. The article said the county police were investigating. He picked up the phone and called his own sheriff.

Counselling, Bassett stormed, post-traumatic stress, what the hell was that? His boys didn't need a shrink. A stable home, fuck. What was wrong with their mother, laying around in that hospital? He hadn't hit her that hard. Now, where would they send the kids? They'd turn the boys against him, those counsellors. They might not send them to foster care. One of those do-gooders would take them.

Maybe that one where Chrissy stays. Nora didn't have no relatives for them to stay with and all he had was that crazy Tabitha, and who knew where she was.

He abandoned the stolen truck in a quarry near the cabin he had broken into and set off through the woods towards a small hamlet on the way back to Culver's. He passed two homes with no vehicles in front or their garages, but the third one had a newer SUV in the lane. Country people, still feeling safe, left the keys in the ignition. He was on his way.

As he drove closer to Culver's Mills, Bassett tried to plan a way to find his sons. That doctor knew where they were, he thought.

She treated them, the paper said. He thought it said that. Why'd he tear it up? He coulda read it again. It said where she was staying.

Bassett's mind struggled, going off on internal tirades against the police, his wife, Chrissy, blaming them all for his problems. At last, he remembered. She was staying at that bed and breakfast place on Posthill Road. That was on the outskirts of town. He could park the SUV and walk up and have a look.

~

Catherine and Anne were working in the garden under the watchful eye of a uniformed policewoman borrowed by Adam from the county. The lane behind offered cover for Bassett as he paused behind the overgrown lilacs in the fence row. Fuck, he thought, cops. He stood listening. Their voices carried to him, as they called back and forth from where each was working. They were talking about the newspaper article.

"Did you read what Ted wrote about you in the paper yesterday?" Catherine asked.

"Yes, and I am so annoyed with him. He made it sound as though I was in charge of their case. All I did was tell him about post-traumatic stress disorder in general. I didn't say I was treating the boys. It would have been an appalling breach of confidentiality if I had. I have to ask him to print an explanation."

Anne knelt at the edge of the garden, punctuating her words with angry stabs at the ground with her trowel.

"Lucky that's a weed in front of you and not Ted," Catherine said.

"Well, how could he? What will Thomas think if he reads it?"

"Are you going to call him about it?"

"No, I'll speak to Ted about it."

"What happened to those Bassett boys? "

Anne, who did, said she had no idea.

"Karen," Catherine asked the policewoman, "are those little

boys okay? Did they have to go to foster care? I could take them for a few days if there's a need."

"Thanks, but they're fine. A relative is looking after them."

Crap, thought Bassett. They ain't no relatives. He trudged back towards the SUV. If he could find Chrissy, she'd tell him, or he'd beat it out of her. He set off for the house of the "do-gooder".

Ada and Chrissy had finished a morning of gardening by getting out Ada's old wicker chairs and sprucing them up with a 'lick of white paint' as Ada put it.

"Let's have lunch, Chrissy," Ada said, turning to her young helper. At the look of fear on Chrissy's face, she whirled to the street. Gord Bassett lumbered towards them; his huge fists curled at his sides.

"Where the hell are your brothers, bitch?"

"Like I would tell you."

"You will if you don't want this interfering old bag to get hurt."

Bassett grabbed Ada by her arm and shook her like a bag of laundry. Chrissy flew at him, pounding him with her small fists. With his free arm, he pushed her in the chest and sent her flying across the lawn.

"Where are they?"

He shook Ada again.

"They're at Aunt Tabby's. Don't hurt Ada anymore."

"Where does she live?"

"I don't know. I haven't been to see them yet."

"Do you want me to hit this old woman?"

"I don't know. I don't know. Don't hurt her."

Bassett released Ada, who stumbled and fell across one of the lawn chairs. Chrissy ran to Ada, who told her she was all right and to go call 911 and tell them what had happened. Bassett's SUV skidded around the corner and out of sight.

Adam was back in his office when the call came through from the northern sheriff. It sure sounded like Bassett was on the move, but it had taken all day for the news to filter down to him. Adam called Bill at the County Sheriff's office. Bassett must have stolen a vehicle. The shopkeeper said it was a battered red truck, but no one reported a theft.

The desk receptionist buzzed him as he was putting on his jacket to leave.

"Adam, there's a 911 call about a guy terrorizing Ada Warren. The young girl who made the call sounded frantic, the operator says. They dispatched. The man had left by the time the girl called, but she says he's her stepfather and he's looking for her brothers. And there's a kid here who insists on talking to you."

Chapter Thirty-Six

Kyle reached for a branch of the walnut tree that hung low over the fence around his aunt's backyard. He was going to be late, and Aunt Tabby would be mad if he didn't make it on time. He crept onto the branch and dropped into the yard. As he ran up to the back door, he heard a man's voice yelling. Who could be there? It didn't sound like his dad. He was still scared that his dad would come and hurt Tabitha, no matter how much she reassured him.

"Make the call, lady," the voice said.

Kyle crept onto the porch and along under the windows to the living room. He raised his head and peered in. Tabitha and Mike huddled together on the couch, staring up at a man who waved a gun at them.

"Make the call or the kid gets it."

Kyle stood against the wall of the porch, trying to stop trembling and trying to think. He'd find Davidson. He let them stay with Aunt Tabby. He was okay. If he ran to the police station, he could find him in time.

He set off running faster that he had ever run before, across lawns and through back alleys to get to the square. As he disappeared around the corner, an SUV parked in the lane behind Tabitha's property and a man got out, leaving the door open behind him. A few seconds work opened the locked gate. He slipped through and ran across the yard. Bassett had found his boys.

A young boy stood in front of the receptionist's desk, his hands clenched into tight little fists, and his eyes fixed on the door. When he saw Adam, he raced across to him, blurting out his story and his fear.

"Hold it, Kyle. Slow down and tell me what's going on."

"Lieutenant, we got a call from his aunt. Some guy is holding a gun on her and the other boy, demanding the paintings and a helicopter out of here."

"Some guy? Do you know who it is?" Adam asked as he put his arm around the trembling boy.

"Is it your dad?"

"No, I never saw him before. We gotta go there, Lieutenant. We gotta save them."

Kyle sobbed into his sleeve.

"We're going. You stay here with Kelly and Dr. McPhail.

"Anne, can you stay with him?"

"Sure."

Anne put her hand on Kyle's shoulder as they watched the policemen leave.

Inside Tabitha's home, the gunman waited, pacing the length of the small room. Two hours he gave them. Small town cops. Could they make a decision or would they call in FBI or some state police? He wanted that painting. Four years of planning. Three years living in this god-forsaken little town. He'd earned it. And now he wouldn't have to share any of it. That bitch last night threatening him, wanting it all her way. She deserved what she got.

What was wrong with that kid? The boy froze, staring at something he had seen through the open door. Could they be in the house so soon? The kid looked terrified.

He edged back to the wall, using the width of the door to shield himself from the opening. He darted a glance at Mike. Now the kid was hiding his face in his aunt's shoulder. Maybe he didn't see nothing.

"Hey, kid, what did you see?"

"What?"

"What did you see through the door?"

"Nothing."

Bassett had moved back into the kitchen and crept out to his vehicle. A shotgun hung on the rack in the back window. Sirens grew closer.

Adam set up his line at the edge of Tabitha's lawn and waited.

Inside the man with the gun paced. Christ, the cops were here already. If he talked to them, they would try to talk him out. The phone rang.

"Lady, you talk to them."

He waved the gun at Tabitha.

"Hello?"

"Tabitha, it's Adam Davidson. Are you all right? Who's with you?"

"Mike. I don't know where Kyle is."

"He's at the station. He saw the situation and came to us. He's frightened but not hurt. Put the guy on."

"He won't talk to you," she told him, after offering the phone to her guard.

"Tell him if he doesn't talk to me, no deal."

Adam heard her pass on his message, and then the phone went dead.

Inside, the phone hit the wall, knocking a picture to the floor. The sound of shattering glass mingled with Mike's screams. He whimpered as he clutched at his aunt.

"Now what?" Tabitha said.

"Shut up; I have to think."

Outside, Adam took a call from Kelly.

After Adam had left, Anne had tried to distract the frantic Kyle by getting out her drawing materials. She took her pencils and sketch pad from her bag and asked him if he would like to draw. When he refused, Anne started drawing the objects on the desk, hoping he would get interesting.

"This is strange," Kelly, the deputy guarding them, said to Anne.

"What's strange?"

"The prints from Janice Maynard's apartment belong to a guy."

"Did they only find one set?"

"Yes."

"May I see?" holding out her hand for the fax.

The thin face, delicate for a man, no or little facial hair, illuminated by large dark eyes, belonged to a man called Raymond Charron, known to be involved with art theft but also suspected of several vicious assaults. You never knew, Anne thought, from the way a person looked. Although, there was an odd look in that man's eyes. She'd seen it before, in the eyes of autistic children; a look that said the rest of the world didn't quite exist. The face looked a little familiar to her.

"Kelly, can you make some copies for me?"

"Sure."

Kyle came around the desk to look at the picture.

"That's the man, Dr. McPhail. That's the man who has Aunt Tabitha and Mike."

"Are you sure, Kyle?"

"Yes, yes."

Kelly started across the room to radio Adam.

Anne took her charcoal from her bag and added a hat to one of the copies. Not the face that trembled at the edge of her memory. She added a moustache—no. More hair, perhaps.

She added short curls, then a big, bouffant hair do. The face of Janice Maynard looked back at her.

"Kelly, Kelly, tell him that guy is Janice Maynard."

"What?"

"Look at this picture."

Adam answered the call. Kelly's excited voice came through. "Lieutenant, that man's name is Raymond Charron. Kyle recognized the picture."

"What picture?"

"The identification picture from the fingerprints from Maynard's apartment. They are the same as the ones at Matilde's place. Anne drew a big hairdo around the picture and this guy Charron is Maynard or at least her twin."

"Send the picture."

Adam picked up his megaphone. "Charron, you need to talk to me. Pick up that phone."

Charron thought Bassett. He was a crazy bastard. The cops would try to wait him out, but he'd kill them. Kill his boy. He had to get him. He edged down the hall from the kitchen. Mike was crying again.

His shotgun blast hit Charron low, too low. Charron fell but didn't lose his grip on the gun. He lay quietly, waiting for the shooter to come in sight.

Bassett walked into the room, cradling his shotgun. "Come on, Mike. We're getting out of here.

"No, I want to stay with Aunt Tabby. We're going to see my mom."

"You're coming with me. Where's Kyle?"

"I don't know. I don't want to go." Mike sobbed and clung to his aunt.

Charron's finger tightened on the trigger. His shot hit Bassett in the back, spun him around. Bassett fell, blood oozing from his spine and trickling from the corner of his mouth. A dead eye stared up at Mike. He screamed, and his aunt turned his face away.

Outside, Adam heard the first shot, shouted "Go, go." into his radio.

Brad hit the front door first with the full force of his heavy shoulders.

"Police," shouted Adam as he ran down the hall toward the living room. Charron raised his pistol and waited.

Coming in from the rear, one of the team, Dave Graham, shot Charron in the chest. When Adam reached him, he was dead.

The room filled with massive men in helmets and body armor. A stricken Dave sat beside Charron's body.

"Lieutenant, he was going to shoot you."

"It's okay. You did what you had to do." Adam went to Tabitha and Mike and led them outside to the waiting paramedics. Finally over, he thought, finally over.

Chapter Thirty-Seven

The next day brought some good news. Pete was going to be fine. No bones were broken, and the wound was clean with no infection so far. Trevelyan and Mrs. Bassett made slow but steady recoveries. Chrissy and Tabitha and the boys were visiting when Adam stopped by.

"Lieutenant," Nora Bassett said, putting out her hand.

Adam took the pale, cool hand between his.

"How are you doing, Nora?"

Her battered face, missing teeth and multicolored from the bruising, smiled up at him.

"'I'm fine now. Thank you for saving my family."

"You're welcome, but the boys did a lot to save themselves, and my staff did the hard work."

"I know you tried to get me to leave him, but I was so afraid."

Her eyes filled with tears.

"He hurt me so much, and he threatened to kill Chrissy if I left. He would have."

"You're going to be fine now," said. "I'll help you all I can."

"Tabitha has been so kind."

"Yes, she has." He stood up to go. "I'll drop in again."

He left, planning to tell Dave Graham, who still reeled from the shooting, how his actions helped this family.

Anne came into the station to finish her work on the Leclerc genealogy. She arranged to meet Nancy Webb at Evan's for dinner and wanted to give her a copy. Both Nancy and Trevelyan would be unhappy with the results, she thought. Land records recorded a sale by the legitimate heir in 1875 that took the piece of property out of Leclerc hands. Anne wanted to see the pictures stolen from the library. They were returned to Evan's since there was no legal case pending.

"Adam," she asked, "would you join Nancy and Catherine and Erin and me for dinner at Evan's. We're going to view the pictures at last. Thomas may be able to join us as well."

"Nancy?"

"She wants to understand about her family."

"And try to get some cash, likely."

"Give her a chance."

"Okay, okay. What time?"

"Seven."

A cold wind blew across the square and swirled around Anne and Catherine at Evan's front door. Mary and Andre took them into the dining room where Adam and Erin sat in front of the fire, sipping wine and looking at the painting and sampler. Andre displayed them on easels where the ceiling lights would best illuminate them.

A few moments later, Nancy arrived, and Thomas followed her.

"Adam, I have been wondering why the paintings were moved so often," Thomas said after joining the group sitting in front of the fireplace.

"Dishonor among thieves. There's no one alive to ask, but we think it went like this. First, they stashed the crates here, convenient for Matilde to watch over them. Next, they moved them to the farm when Mary and Andre went to New York, to wait for transit somewhere else. When Bassett went missing, the thieves took them to the farm. Matilde couldn't resist having a browse around Evan's and didn't count on Mary being so observant."

"Why were you so frightened?" Anne asked, turning to Nancy.

"I felt responsible. There was so much suspicion of me the first time when Jennifer's body was found in my library, that I was sure I would be suspected this time. Whenever I saw Adam, I was sure he was going to arrest me."

Anne put her hand over Nancy's restless fingers, twisting her napkin into knots.

"Try to relax; you're safe now."

Mary and Andre joined them for dessert, and the discussion turned to the painting and sampler.

Samuel Leclerc's eyes, gazing out from the portrait, met Anne's.

"You have Samuel's eyes," she said to Nancy.

She went on to show Nancy her genealogy and how her mother's family fit into the long line from Samuel. Nancy and Trevelyan were remote cousins.

"How is he?" Nancy asked. "I'll go visit him."

"He's coming along, but the doctor said it would take a long time," Adam said.

Anne said, "This painting isn't good enough to explain all this killing or the theft."

She got up and walked around the easel.

"Can I carry it to better light," she asked Andre.

"Sure."

The weight of the painting surprised her. She had examined many old paintings in her prowls through antique stores. This one was too heavy, and its back was covered with cardboard, not rare but also unusual.

"Erin, heft this. Do you think this picture is too heavy?"

"Yes, it is."

"Can we dismantle your painting," Adam asked Andre as he threw his arm around Anne's shoulders, "otherwise I don't think she will ever be satisfied."

"I'll get pliers."

When Andre pulled off the thick backing, a canvas, no more than ten inches by twelve inches, fell into his hands. A bright landscape, resplendent with sunflowers and poplars, expanded under a turbulent sky. The signature in the corner, read, in printed letters, Vincent.

"Could it be real?" Erin said.

"I hope so. I'll check the stolen art list. Thank you, Dr. McPhail," Adam said, hugging her.

"You're welcome. There's one other thing."

"Not something behind the sampler?"

"No, I don't think so, but you might check. It's Samuel and the way he's pointing to those objects on the mantelpiece, and then there's the figure in the sampler. I mean, why the shovel?" A stylized spade leaned against a tree. "Is the tree still there?"

"Yes, it is," said Andre. "Shall we dig now or in the morning?"

In the morning, the group stood around the oak. The figure in the sampler pointed to the ground, to the right of the tree and about three feet away. Erin cautioned that there was no true rendering of distance in folk-art of this type.

"Andre, dig next to the tree but try to compensate for the growth," Anne said.

Two hours and four holes later, they were about to give up when Adam's shovel hit something metallic. He unearthed a metal box, locked, with an SL etched into the top.

Andre had a collection of old keys he found in the drawer in the house. With the help of a little oil, one opened the box.

"It looks like the ring, the candlestick, a small cup, a small square of metal that looks like gold and a little wooden box," Andre said.

"What's in the box?" someone asked.

That was the most exciting; a letter from Paul Revere to his dear friend Samuel, sending him a pewter tankard, made by himself on the occasion of Samuel's son's birth.

Chapter Thirty-Eight

Anne closed the trunk of her car and embraced Catherine.

"Good-bye. Good luck with university."

Catherine had decided to return to school, hoping to study law.

"Thank you. Thanks for everything, Anne, especially for your help with the boys. Enjoy your visit to Bermuda but don't find any more bodies."

"I shall try to avoid it."

About the Author

Virginia Winters was born in Arnprior, Ontario, Canada and raised in the Ottawa Valley. After high school in Renfrew, another Valley town, she went down to Queens to study medicine, graduating in 1970. Fellowship in Pediatrics followed, with graduation in 1976. That year she and her husband, Internist George Winters, moved to Lindsay, Ontario with their two children, and have lived there ever since. Virginia's interests, besides writing, are genealogy, gardening, photography, and studying languages (currently Spanish). The Facepainter Murders is the second in the Dangerous Journeys series.

Murderous Roots , Virginia Winters's first novel, an e- book, was published on December 1, 2009 by Write Words Inc. and is now available in paper from that press and at Amazon.com.

Short works have appeared on-line in Camroc Press Review, Six Sentences, and Pine Tree Mysteries and most recently in the Gumshoe Review. Short stories have been published in Confabulation2 and 3, anthologies produced by Wynterblue Publishing, North Bay, Ontario.

Virginia blogs about writing and other interests, including genealogy, current events and gardening.

For more information or to contact Virginia:
virginiawinters.ca
vwinters@bell.net

If you enjoyed The Facepainter Murders, please consider leaving a line or two of review on Amazon. Reviews are important to indie authors to get the word out about a book or a series. There are now 5 books in the series Dangerous Journeys and a collection of short stories, some featuring Anne McPhail.

No Motive for
Murder

BOOK 3

Virginia Winters

Chapter 1

Sudden rain battered Bermuda that morning, pounding the whitewashed roof on its way to the cistern. Rivulets coursed down the windows. The wind bent the old trees that stood in front of the house, survivors of hurricanes of the last fifty years. Beyond the trees, whitecaps crashed against the grey dock and up onto the white stones stacked along the shore. Anne turned from the window when she saw the car arrived. Usually, she took the bus when she went anywhere without her sister, but this was a taxi sort of day.

A sweeping drive led off the street and around an immense ornamental pond to Hamilton's city hall. At the top of the welcoming arms staircase, two-story white pillars guarded the doors. A replica of the ship Discovery decorated the summit of the clock tower, gleaming in the sudden sunshine. Below it, the clock with its sea-blue face chimed ten o'clock.

Wide Bermuda cedar stairs, carpeted in deep red, led up from the foyer to an encircling mezzanine. Anne paused to admire the portraits of a young Queen Victoria and Prince Albert, copies of the Winterhalter oils that hung in Windsor Castle that flanked the entrance to the National Art Gallery.

She spent a pleasant but solitary two hours in the permanent collection of paintings, furniture and objets d'arte made by Bermuda artists or inspired by the islands. At noon, she thanked the volunteer at the desk and signed the guest book. There was still time to see an exhibition of art by local children that hung in a room at the other end of the mezzanine. She opened the door.

A scene from a movie. The sound effect, a muffled explosion. One man down, the other searching his pockets. She, screaming, frozen for a moment.

He heard her, jerked his head towards her and away and fled through the exit door. She raced across the endless meters that separated her from the young black man crumpled on the floor.

She pulled off her jacket and knelt by his body; blood was spurting from the hole in his navy tee shirt. The wound punctuated the proud words written on his shirt—Bermuda Born. So young she thought. So young. The soft white cotton of her jacket, pressed against his chest, turned red beneath her hands. His fading heart fluttered and stopped; colour faded from his lips; the pupils in his dark brown eyes dilated. She started chest compressions, but she knew it was too late. The bullet must have gone straight to his heart.

He had no chance. No chance.

"Help," she screamed again. "Help me!"

Blood seeped from beneath the body and congealed on her yellow linen skirt—a thickening, dull-red jelly. A man in a grey uniform, perhaps a security guard, appeared at the top of the staircase, ran towards her along the blue carpet, stopped, his mouth opened to speak, and then he wheeled into the Art Gallery.

Where was he going? Couldn't he see she was in trouble?

A woman appeared in the gallery door, the volunteer from the desk inside, gasped and disappeared.

"Stop. Come back."

Hours passed, or so it seemed. The movements developed an automatic rhythm, useless, but automatic. Sweat dripped into her eyes, and her shoulders ached. Her own heart beat a frantic rhythm too, but she couldn't stop; didn't want to let him go. The iron smell of blood, mixed with a fecal stench rose from the body. She gagged and turned aside, afraid she would vomit into the wound, and then started again. At last two paramedics reached her and one took her place on the body. A few people—the volunteer from the gallery, the security guard, three others —stood watching from the safety of the gallery door.

Anne sat back against the wall and pulled in her feet, away from the blood that seemed to creep towards her. The man—the shooter —looked back at her when she shouted at him, wrenched something from his victim's hand and ran to the exit: a strange man— white skin and white hair beneath a ball cap. Something odd about his walk, not a limp, exactly. His gait was uneven, a slight hesitation with his right leg. She thought she'd seen him before. But where and when?

She watched the familiar routine of intravenous fluids and cardiogram and heard the final decision that he was gone. A second crew arrived, and another paramedic came to her. Anne stood up to speak to him and then sat down and folded her arms into her suddenly cold body.

"I'm a doctor," she said. "His heart stopped about 11:47."

A uniformed policeman asked her to come with him.

They walked through into the gallery and behind the counter to a small office. Anne sat in a green upholstered chair, opposite a young woman taking notes.

"I'm Deputy-Inspector Spottiswood, of the Serious Crimes Unit," said the woman. "I understand you found the body. May I have your name please?"

"I'm Anne McPhail. I'm a physician. He was alive when I got to him but died moments later."

"Residence?"

The woman kept her head down while she scribbled in a black-covered notebook, the kind workmen used to keep track of their hours. Anne gave her sister's address and added that she was visiting Bermuda from Canada.

"What is your address in Canada?"

Still no eye contact. Was it some investigatory technique, or was the detective just a rude woman? She gave the address of her house in Bridgenorth, in Ontario. She focused on the view of blue sky and white roofs visible through the window behind her questioner. Still, the woman kept her dark head bent, her gaze on the stubby yellow pencil in her hand and on the words she was adding. Her writing was almost printing. She added a star to one line, then another. What did she say that was so important, Anne wondered.

"And your business address?"

"I've retired,"

"Say again."

"I said that I've retired."

"Aren't you a little young for retirement?"

The woman raised one eyebrow, and her gaze flickered towards the constable standing behind Anne.

"Perhaps."

What concern was that to the police? Anne could feel the heat rising in her face and knew it would be flaming red in a few seconds. When was this woman going to get past the irrelevant?

The questions that followed were more of the same: exact details of when she arrived; what pictures she looked at; where she was going when she left, and so on.

"Did you recognize the man who ran away?"

Anne turned to look at the woman and found brown eyes staring into hers. They should have been soft, to match her full mouth and neatly rounded chin, but they were, not hard, but unyielding.

"No, or rather he reminded me of a man I sat beside on the plane yesterday."

"What did he look like?"

"I can describe the man on the plane, but I had only the briefest glimpse of the one who ran out of here this morning. Not enough to swear that it was the same man. He—the man on the plane—was over six feet, the average weight for that height, white hair, thick, pale skin. He could have been albino except his eyes were grey, not blue."

"What reminded you?"

"Just his walk, or rather his run. He pushed past me on the gangway from the plane, and I watched him walk across the tarmac, and it was the same gait, or so I thought. The man who shot the boy was about the same height and weight, and I think his hair was white, but he was wearing a ball cap, so I'm not sure."

"What was wrong with his gait? Was he crippled in some way? Use a cane?"

"None of that. A little hesitation on the right."

"Not enough."

"As I said."

Anne waited again for the yellow pencil to catch up with what she'd said. The view out the window hadn't changed, except for a tiny spot of orange on one roof. Anne watched it creep across the white tiles. A ginger cat she thought, hunting.

"Did you know the victim?"

"No."

She saw a brief change of expression on the other woman's face. She didn't believe her, Anne thought, and her chest tightened.

"We'll need to search you, Doctor."

"What? Why?"

"We have to ascertain whether or not anyone on the scene has a gun. Please go with the constable."

Anne handed over her purse and her raincoat. She was wearing a simple short-sleeved blue shirt and pale yellow skirt, or at least it had been yellow. Little room to conceal a weapon, she thought, but a woman constable took her into the gallery of children's art and waited until she stripped to her underwear and dressed again in a set of hospital greens. At least no body cavity search.

"I need to wash."

232

"We have to check your hands and fingernails, so no washing right now."

"You have no idea whether this young man had an infectious disease."

"Take it up with the Inspector."

The Deputy Inspector started again when they joined her.

"Why are you on Bermuda?"

"Before we go on, I need to clean my hands."

"Soon enough."

"Now."

The inspector looked again at the standing male constable, who left and returned with a scene-of-the-crime technician. When he finished, he handed Anne wipes and disinfectant for her hands.

"Why are you on Bermuda?"

"Visiting my family."

"Why aren't you visiting them?"

"My sister works mornings, and I wanted to visit the gallery. I'm supposed to meet her for lunch. She's called me several times, I'm sure, but you have my cell phone. She'll come looking for me any moment."

"Is your sister a Bermuda citizen?"

Anne wondered what difference that made, but answered, "Yes."

She gave her sister's name and that of her brother-in-law and the name of his business.

"I would like my belongings back now, and I would like to call my sister." She stood up.

"You expect me to take your word for all of it: the man who ran away; the time of death; how long you spent in the gallery."

The detective was standing now, leaning over the desk that separated them.

"As to the last, I spoke to the volunteer on the desk in there, when I went in and said goodbye when I left. I was the only visitor, so perhaps she'll remember me. As to the time of death, the EMS attempted to resuscitate him. I expect they don't try that on the long dead. As to the first, yes you only have my word. When you check on me, you'll find my word is good."

"We'll ask you to surrender your passport, which I see you're not carrying."

"Does Bermuda law require that I carry it at all times?"

"No."

"I'll surrender it after I speak to my consulate and a lawyer. I would like my cell phone back, please."

"We've bagged it as evidence."

"Evidence of what? I would like a receipt."

A uniformed police officer spoke to the detective and handed her an evidence bag.

"Do you recognize this, Doctor McPhail?"

Anne could see a gun, fitted with what she assumed was a silencer, through the dull plastic.

"I know nothing about guns, and I don't recognize that one. I'm a physician, Detective. I don't shoot people. My job is to save them."

"It was found outside the exit door. Why would that mysterious man of yours have left his weapon behind?"

"Again, I have no idea and he's not my man."

"We'll be checking it for fingerprints and DNA."

"You won't find mine."

A constable whispered into Spottiswood's ear.

"Your sister is at the front door. You can go now, Doctor, but don't leave Bermuda. If you try, we will stop you, and we will arrest you."

Anne could sense the other two police in the room watching her, waiting for her reply. She caught a raised- eyebrow glance between the two men.

"Stop threatening me, Deputy Inspector. I did nothing except to find this unfortunate young man. My lawyer will be in touch regarding my passport and my phone."

~

At that Anne turned and stalked past the other two police, under the yellow tape and down the stairs. She could see Liz beyond the front door. A knot of police and others Anne thought were reporters stood between them. A fair-haired woman stepped forward, and the man beside her started his camera recording.

"Doctor McPhail, Doctor McPhail. Can you describe what happened to us? Who was shot? Do you know him?" the English voice demanded.

How the hell did they get her name all ready? Did the police give it to them? Maybe the woman in the gallery?

"No comment," Anne said.

She caught a glimpse of her sister's blonde head through the throng of yelling reporters. Anne turned to a policeman who cleared a path through the crowd for her.

"What happened?" Liz said when Anne reached her. "Are you hurt?"

"No. Get me out of here. I have to talk to you and Dave. I need a lawyer."

Anne forced the words out past a constriction in her throat and willed herself to breathe.

"What happened?" Liz asked again when the car doors closed them in. Her pale brows knitted above worried blue eyes.

"I found a man shot up there. He died before I could do more than try to stop the bleeding. A young man, Liz, no older than Martin."

She brushed away tears and leaned forward into her hands.

"Who was he?" Liz took her hand off the key and waited.

"Drive, drive. I don't want to stay here any longer."

"Who was he?" Liz pulled away from the curb and into the airport traffic.

"I don't know. If the police know, they didn't say. And the investigator, a woman called Spottiswood, is threatening me with arrest if

I try to leave the island. And she wants me to surrender my passport!"

"Can she do that?"

"I have no idea. That's why I have to go to the consulate and get a lawyer."

"I think we have to talk to Dave and Martin."

"That too."

"Do you want to go home first? Clean off the blood?"

Anne pulled down the sun visor. Blood smeared her face and matted the platinum of her hair.

"The police didn't take me to a washroom, even after I was searched. They took scrapings from under my fingernails and swabbed my hands and arms for gunshot residue. They gave me wipes for my hands but said nothing about blood on my face. And then they let me walk out, blood all over me. And someone gave the press my name. The pictures in the newspapers will convict me."

"Don't start, Anne. Don't jump ahead. You're not arrested, after all."

"That woman frightened me."

At Dave's office, the assistant stood up and walked around her desk to shake hands with Liz.

"Madeline, is Dave free? We have to speak to him. This is my sister, Anne McPhail."

"His meeting will be over in a few minutes. I'll tell him that you're here. Can I do anything else for you? Tea?"

Her gaze dropped to Anne's still grubby hands and then her streaked face.

"Something stronger?"

"Tea." Anne sank into a metal armchair. The dark green fabric of the back and seat felt rough through the thin cotton of the hospital greens.

"Do you want to clean up? There's a full bath attached to the office," Liz asked again.

"Yes."

But cleaning up had to wait. Dave opened the door behind the assistant's desk. He towered over her five-foot-two sister. His dark blue eyes, brilliant in his tanned face, narrowed when he saw Anne.

"What's going on? Anne, are you hurt?"

"No, no."

"In your office," Liz commanded.

Dave raised his eyebrows but followed along as she ploughed through the door and along the hall to his expansive corner office. High windows on two sides gave views of the harbor and the city, and let in the light needed for his work. Two junior architects stood over a model of an office building. Dave asked them for a few minutes privacy, and after a glimpse of Anne's face, they scuttled out the door.

"What the hell?"

"Anne found another body."

Liz collapsed into a black leather visitor's chair near Dave's desk. Anne took another. Dave stood in the window, looking, or so it seemed, across the harbor. He was curly-haired and blue-eyed, tanned and cheerful, middle-height and middle-aged. Took care of himself, Anne saw—a little midriff spread but not much—testimony to the benefits of sailing and Bermuda's hilly landscape.

"Where were you?" he asked when he turned around.

"At the art gallery. When I walked out of the gallery, I heard something, like a muffled gunshot. There were two men, one lying on the floor, the other rifling through the fallen man's pockets. When I reached the one on the floor, he was gone. There was nothing I could do for him. He'd been shot, straight through the heart it looked like. I called for help, and the paramedics and the police came. A woman called Spottiswood is the investigator, and she told me not to try to leave the island and said they would want my passport. Can she do that without charging me with anything?"

"You're a witness. She won't want to let you go."

"They found a weapon outside the exit door. She showed it to me. A gun with a tube attached to the barrel, a silencer, I suppose.

"The gun's not connected to you, so try not to worry," Liz said.

"I need to talk to the consulate."

"Ken Marshall's a good solicitor. I'll call him," said Dave.

"I don't understand why I need one. I've done nothing. They did the test to see if I'd fired a gun."

"Accomplice," Dave said.

"What?"

"They may think you're an accomplice."

Wind, whipping torrential rain against her bedroom window, woke Anne the next morning. Black clouds and rain, she thought. Perfect. The weather was tracking her mood. She caught a glimpse of the angry sea through a moon gate in the stacked stone wall that surrounded the property. She jerked the drapes closed. She wanted off the island; wanted to go home to Canada, to her safe little house.

Liz knocked and carried in a jaunty orange tray laden with a white china teapot and two cups. She sat it down on a glass-topped table in front of the window and handed Anne a cup decorated with roses and took one, daisies, for herself, then opened the drapes. She looked casually elegant in a soft blue dress and jacket in a darker shade.

Anne scowled at the open window. "You're up early," she said.

"I have to go to work."

"You're not coming to the lawyer, then? I hoped you would be able to."

She pushed away her cup and gripped her hands together until the knuckles turned white.

"No, but Dave stayed home. He'll go with you."

"I hope the lawyer believes me."

"Whether he does or doesn't, his job is to give you advice."

"If he doesn't, how can I expect the police to?"

"Come on, Anne. You should wait to worry about whether or not he believes you until after you meet him. The office is in Hamilton, but I'll see you at home afterwards. Try to relax a little. This isn't like you."

"It is though. I had the same reaction in Vermont, the first time."

Anne dressed for her meeting in a dark green skirt, celery-colored cotton sweater and a jacket that matched the skirt. She added a single gold chain and wore the ruby and diamond engagement ring that Michael had given her, on her right hand. She struggled a little to get it over the knuckle. Her professional self looked back at her from the mirror. A uniform always helped, she thought.

She sat across the breakfast table from Dave, nibbled toast, and picked at a dish of mango slices and strawberries. He was a man who never sugarcoated anything, so Anne was certain of blunt answers to her questions.

"Is he a criminal lawyer?"

"You mean does he do the courtroom work?"

"Yes."

"No. He would brief the barrister if it were to come to that. He's a good lawyer, Anne. Tough and well- respected."

"I still can't believe I'm in this position. What is wrong with that woman? Why did she leap to the conclusion that I must be involved, without knowing the first thing about me?"

"I don't know anything about her, but the lawyer might. We should get going."

Sunshine had replaced the wind and rain by the time they left the house. Anne loved the quirky streets in Bermuda: the circular mirrors mounted at intersections; the stone walls, draped in flowers; the morning glories climbing the telephone poles and creeping out along the wires. The street names intrigued her—Flowercote Lane was a favorite. That morning she didn't see any of them.

~

The lawyer's office inhabited the penthouse level of a four-story building on Church Street. The architect must have been striving for a Caribbean look, Anne thought, judging by the balconies that punctuated the facade, and the deep-set windows, Small projections from the roof-line, on the other hand, suggested a gesture towards the crenelations of English castles. Perhaps it was a new school, Interpretive Caribbean Architecture, or some such.

They took the elevator to the third floor and walked up to the fourth. The foyer, guarded by a single receptionist, opened into a large room, filled with light and sunshine from the tall windows on three sides. Low partitions separated the space into cubicles. Law books lined the walls between and under the windows. The four partners' offices were along the remaining side, with the two seniors in the corners and the juniors in the center.

The lawyer, Ken Marshall, furnished his space in an old-fashioned way—dark wood furniture and bookshelves, comfortable leather chairs for himself and the client. Pictures of his family occupied a shelf in one corner, visible from his spot behind the desk.

He took the details in the old way too, longhand on a legal-sized yellow pad. Was there a whole industry devoted to creating these pads for lawyers all over the world, Anne wondered, or just Western ones? She liked him: his handshake; his reading glasses, pulled from a desk drawer when she started her story; his deep voice.

"Can they take my passport? And should I speak to the consulate?"

"Yes, they can take your passport, but let's wait for an official request. The consulate should know about the trouble. Their office in New York handles Bermuda, but there is an on-island Honorary Consul. I'll call her. If she wants or needs to see you, I'll let you know."

He was taking charge in his lawyerly way, but that meant she would get her money's worth, not that she would be safe.

"I told the detective you would be in touch."

"Clients say and do many things without discussing it with us first. We can ignore that. Don't speak to them again without me there."

"Do I have the right to ask that you be contacted if they arrest me or take me in for questioning?"

"Yes, you do, if you were arrested. If they ask you to come in for questioning, call me before you go. If they take you, but don't give you time to call, say nothing whatsoever but to ask that I be called."

"Won't they think I'm guilty of something if I behave like that."

There was that case of the nurse in Ontario accused of murdering babies. The press and the crown attorney used the fact that she asked for a lawyer immediately as evidence of guilt. And her roommate was a lawyer. Kafka would have understood.

"Answering questions without advice is dangerous. I urge you to call me."

"I will."

He handed her his card, wrote a night phone number on the back, and got down to the business of a retainer, which they paid at the desk. Anne's hand shook a little as she signed the credit card slip for the five-figure fee.

"Do I get some of this back it was to turn out that I didn't need much legal help?" she asked.

"Oh yes," said clerk.

On the way down in the elevator, Dave told Anne not to expect to see much of the ten thousand again.

His son, Martin, met them at the door when they reached home.

"Dad, the dead guy is Nathan Smith."

"Nathan Smith?"

"You remember. We looked at his paintings last weekend at the fair. The news said the police thought the death was drug-related. He was a good guy. He didn't do drugs."

Anne could hear the outrage in his voice.

"You know they always say that now. Was he a good friend? I don't remember you talking about him."

"No. We knew some of the same people. He lived at home with his mother and worked on one of the big estates as a gardener, and he painted."

Martin had dark curly hair and sea-blue eyes like his father and a mouth that was serious most of the time. His smiles were rare, sudden and dazzling. Not that day.

"I should visit his mother. I'm sure she would want to know that he didn't suffer," Anne said.

"I don't think the police would like that," Dave said.

"Why not?"

"Collusion between witnesses."

"For God's sake, Dave. His mother and the woman who held him as he died. You can't be serious."

Anne paced the length of the room, paused to gaze at the Sound for a few seconds and turned back towards the others.

Liz came in from the kitchen and said, "What's all this uproar about?"

"I want to talk to the boy's mother, and Dave thinks the police wouldn't like it."

"You have to be careful, Anne. You're not at home."

"I'm beginning to understand that."

"A bike turned into the driveway," Martin said. "Are we expecting someone?"

"No."

A tiny black woman parked her bike and stood for a moment, looking away from the house towards the Sound, letting the onshore wind blow into her face. She turned and walked up the stairs to the front door. Liz waited for the doorbell to ring and then a few seconds more before she opened it.

"I'm Margaret Smith, Nathan's mother. Could I speak to Doctor McPhail?"

"Yes, of course."

She sat on the sofa, a dark figure in sweater and slacks. A pair of red barrettes in the corn rows that marched across her fine-boned head betraying a taste for color. Perhaps these were her only clothes that weren't vibrant, Anne thought. She sat down beside her and waited in silence. Liz brought in tea and only then did Mrs. Smith speak; her voice heavy and weighed with sadness and tears.

"The police said you were with my boy when he died."

"Yes, I was."

"That detective, Spottiswood, she told me not to talk to you. Why did she say that? Does she think you killed Nathan."

Her voice trembled and her eyes searched Anne's face.

"I didn't, Mrs. Smith. I'm a doctor from Canada. I came to visit my family. I was only at the gallery to look at the art." Anne leaned forward and touched the woman's large-knuckled hand.

"So was Nathan," she said.

Her tears overflowed her eyes and coursed down her cheeks. Anne waited.

When Mrs. Smith was calmer, she said to Anne, "Tell me what happened."

"I came out of the art gallery and saw two men on the mezzanine. One of them slumped to the floor, and the other ran out through the exit. I saw that Nathan was bleeding badly from the wound in his chest, and I tried to help him. He wasn't conscious, and if he suffered, it was only for a moment.

A guard came and looked and a woman from the gallery. They must have called the emergency services because the paramedics came and then the police."

"You don't know who did it?"

"No. I only had a brief glimpse of his face."

"Was he a white man?"

The image of the man's face, his dead white skin under a navy-blue ball cap with its New York Yankees logo, came into focus in her memory.

"Yes. Yes, he was."

"Do you have any idea who would want to kill him?"

"No. There's a girl at Tucker's Point."

Anne knew that the ultra-rich from many countries kept homes in the exclusive enclave of Tucker's Point.

"How did he meet her?" Anne asked.

"He works on her family's estate. He wanted to have some connection to the land that should have been ours."

She lifted her head to look at Dave, as though he would understand.

"What do you mean?" he asked.

"Nathan and I have been searching the land records and the genealogy records for years, trying to find what happened to the land our ancestors owned here."

"Sold?" Dave asked.

"No. No. We couldn't find anything about a sale, and my grand-mother told me the land was stolen from us. I'm not very good at this research and Nathan was more interested in his art. After he met Candice, he told me not to worry, that the land would be ours when he married her. He was such a dreamer."

"Was he seeing Candice Wainwright?" Martin said

"Yes."

"He was dreaming. Her father wouldn't let her marry a local."

"How could he stop it?" Liz asked.

"He'd cut her off. Money is very important to Candice. She would never marry anyone without her daddy's approval."

"Nathan told me they were in love," Nathan's mother said.

Anne saw Liz give Martin a little kick and a look that told him to stop talking.

"Maybe Anne could help you with your research," Dave said. "She has a lot of experience."

"I don't know anything about Bermuda genealogy," Anne said.

"You know how to dig."

"That would be wonderful. I want to know," Margaret said. "I want to know if Nathan and I were right. I don't expect to get any land back. Could you help me?"

"Perhaps. I'll let you know," Anne said.

Margaret was satisfied with that. Dave called her a taxi and waited outside with her until it arrived.

"What were you thinking?" Anne asked Dave when he came back in the house. "When I start to look at someone else's genealogy, I always get into some trouble."

"If the land should belong to her, it would be helpful to know that."

"Helpful to whom?"

"To you. As a motive for murder that doesn't involve you."